so fly

so fly

giselle zado wasfie

ST. MARTIN'S GRIFFIN NEW YORK

This novel is a work of fiction. All of the characters, places, and events portrayed in this book are products of the author's imagination or are used fictitiously. Though real-life celebrities are mentioned in these pages, it should not be inferred that these people participated in or granted their authorization or endorsement of this novel.

www.stmartins.com

ISBN 0-312-33325-0
EAN 978-0312-33325-6

First Edition: May 2005

10 9 8 7 6 5 4 3 2 1

To Mom, Dad, and Nissan,

for their endless encouragement and love

acknowledgments

Up front, I must say thanks be to God for giving me a voice and a space in which I can express myself.

This book was my wish, but without the support of the following people, it wouldn't have come true.

My lovely, faithful agent and friend, Sita White, who saw the spark in my idea years ago and who stuck with me through thick and thin, always with a smile.

My talented, smart editor at St. Martin's Press, Elizabeth Bewley, whose keen eye and enthusiasm took this book to the next level.

All my friends who've been so supportive along the way: in particular, Roxanna Font, founder of Smallwood, where the first chapter was written; Cammie Puidokas, Elaine Oberlin, and Ally Keller, for their thoughtful readings and comments; and Rob Trostle, for his designer talents on the Web site (gisellezadowasfie.com).

My giant, loving family all around the world, for being my best fans and being so proud of me.

All my creative writing professors at the University of Michigan, particularly Kimberly Kafka, whose guidance got me writing fiction and whose faith kept me going after early rejection.

The NYC magazine community and especially the editors who've supported my writing, particularly Alison Brower, for being a mentor and friend, and Sara Nelson, for giving me my first editorial job at *Glamour*.

To the NYC hip-hop community, in particular Steven and Felicia at SOHH.com, Adam Matthews and Hyun Kim, for hiring me way back when, Rakaa Iriscience (Los Angeles), Leah Rose, Jean Grae, Slug and Jbird (Minneapolis), Kevin Powell, the D&D Studios family, and the mighty Chuck D, for always returning my e-mails.

And lastly, many thanks to the myriad musicians, rappers, deejays, and artists who constantly move and inspire me. Without you, my world, and definitely this book, would be a very empty place.

Now girl you too smart to be a tour mark,
Set to play correct from the start with your pure heart

And when you're all alone, I'll sing into your phone
If you don't know the words you can make up your own

–ATMOSPHERE, "Reflections," *Seven's Travels*

so fly

about to merc

In 1998, on the heels of my graduation from the University of Michigan and after a particularly exuberant episode of *Oprah,* I sat on the arm of my hand-me-down couch and made a list entitled "The Top Three Things I Love Most (Besides God)." The third thing I loved most was music.

So right then and there, I managed to make a very big decision. Prompted by the about-to-be-an-alumna "So what are you going to do now?" questions I had been dodging on a daily basis, I decided to leave behind the first and second things I loved most and move to big, bad New York City to pursue a music career.

Smoking a pack a day for five years had flattened my once-pleasurable alto voice; laziness had derailed my piano playing at *The Young and the Restless* theme song and halted my guitar potential at power chords; thus the only realistic option left for my happenin' and currently very imaginary career might be for me to *write* about music. Writing being the thing that, besides chain-smoking, I was consistently good at and wanted to do.

I made that fateful decision to go in search of my pearl, and then I put Ben Harper's acoustic "I Shall Not Walk Alone" on repeat and cried like a little baby. I couldn't tell if it was because I was happy or sad to go, but the tears came sporadically throughout the night: when I'd hung up the phone with my mom, while I was washing my face in the shower, and even after Ryan and I made out and he fell asleep next to me while the *Edward Scissorhands* soundtrack spun delicate webs on my antique gramophone.

In my twin bed, I traced the scar on Ryan's shoulder that looked like a crafty grandma's cross-stitch. Then, I pressed my lips on it and our skin slowly parted like peeling tape. I wondered, in those minutes, if I'd ever find another guy who didn't mind that sometimes I was too lazy to wax my legs, who tolerated my bizarre need to watch repeated episodes of *Boy Meets World* (love those Savage brothers), who didn't think it was weird that I didn't do any drugs and only drank socially (and who managed to get me sober to go home with him anyway).

A great one-of-a-kind guy who accepted that I wasn't ready to have sex yet; who didn't make fun of me when I raged along with Public Enemy (well a little, but not in a *mean* way) while we cruised down I-75; a boy who seemed to say, "I love you and you don't weird me out." Or, in my more romantic, literary moments, "I see you, Sophie—with and without context—and I still love you."

A guy who tolerated that I couldn't love him back the exact same way, with passion tantamount, and might never.

I felt bad about that last part a lot. Looking for those missing feelings for Ryan was like constantly losing my keys.

I lay there clutching the soft, ratty quilt up to my chin, imagining the monstrous Manhattan skyline and wanting, as Nietzsche so eloquently put it, to become what I am. Or, as we snowboarders say at the top of a mountain, *go big*.

I pictured a glamorous life whereby I rubbed ashen elbows with my favorite musicians and could find out firsthand what made them what they were. I'd ask them questions like, "What made you so mad that you wrote that song?" and "Did you ever see your father again?" or "Do you still love her?"

(Maybe I'd even bed—I mean be*friend*—a couple of them!)

Musicians were fascinating creatures. I wanted some of their inspiration to rub off on me. I yearned to know where their art grew, their nonchalance, indifference to responsibility, and unapologetic self-expression. I coveted their profound disregard for becoming something respectable like a doctor or lawyer. I longed for some of their courage to drip on me. The most adventurous and revealing thing I'd done in college was run the Naked Mile.

I hoped to say thanks, too. Let other people into their mysterious world. Into the sheer joy and unfailing companionship of music, those notes and stories and melodies born from silence that carry us through tough times, connect us to strangers at a concert.

It seemed like very far—planets—between that world and this tiny space with Ryan in it. But, the thought that the other world existed and that I could be something to connect the two made me happy—and petrified.

My trillion thoughts finally exhausted me enough to knock me out and in the morning, it was just another hazy day in a college town and I was still the same girl I'd always been. At least, for a few more weeks until my parents and younger brother drove me to Detroit Metro (my mom did a rosary the whole way) and then said a long good-bye to me by the gate to LaGuardia. I clutched my boarding pass in my hand and wobbled down the hall to the plane, but refused to give in and look back at my family.

I had no idea what I was in for or where I'd end up, but the thing was, I knew I couldn't stay. In my heart, I was already gone.

the jump

Three hours and one scary taxicab experience later, I was making my New York debut as the current couch guest of an old friend/aspiring actress from elementary school named Lucy Arregio. She'd taken me in for $50 a week.

Instantly knee-deep into my gypsy phase and luggage, my "exciting" life in the city seemed nowhere to be found. I realized that somehow my dreams, which had all taken place in the Big Apple, actually felt closer when I was back in Michigan. How was that possible?

Thankfully, Lucy had been mostly sweet since I'd landed. We spent that first evening together eating greasy pizza, watching John Cusack as the incomparable Lloyd Dobler in *Say Anything,* and yapping about the whereabouts of old high school classmates; all the while downing tequila shots, exaggerating details, and happily piecing together second- and third-hand accounts of marriages, new jobs, and even babies.

Lucy spent her days temping at a casting agency and going to auditions, so I was left to the empty railroad apartment and my ho-hum self. Basically, the way I broke it down, I was becoming my new best friend.

I shuffled around the apartment in my slippers and looked through stuff like the pastel tablets in Lucy's medicine cabinet to pass time. I invented a game called "Find A Cigarette" where I'd have to search bookshelves and nooks-'n'-crannies to locate her secret stash of international smokes like Rothmans and YSLs and Gitanes.

I felt weird about polishing off the cookie dough ice cream in the freezer, playing Lucy's stereo too loud, and using her Tom's Toothpaste, but she swore in two languages (*"mi casa es su casa"*) that I should make myself at home, so I'd done all three before 11 a.m., which quickly left me on the prowl for more mid-day activities.

The best part of the past forty-eight hours had been Lucy's computer and the Internet, where I fished for hope. I checked out obscure job listings, e-mailed handfuls of people with my résumé, and corresponded with my brother who reminded me I had to be patient through the process.

"I'm sure it's tough," he wrote. "That's why everyone wants to live in New York, but instead just reads stories or listens to songs or watches films about it. Stop the drama and get your piece of the action. You can do it."

I'm sure this detached way of looking at things and positive reinforcement was supposed to make me feel less alone, but when I clicked REPLY and started typing, all my doubts overflowed:

"I might have made a mistake coming here. I don't know what to do with myself and my savings is already starting to dwindle. It's like it just automatically costs $20 a day to live here, even if you don't buy anything. What was I thinking? I'll never get my foot in the door. I feel lost. Alone. Dumb. Fat."

Send.

I pried myself off the seat and walked to the couch. I didn't know why I'd just told my brother I felt bloated. None of the unsavory states were exclusive to my moving away, and he really couldn't solve them if they were.

I slapped a tape in the stereo, headed for the bathroom, and turned on the shower. It was 1:30 p.m. After the water cleansed me and I came out smelling like baby powder, I felt refreshed and ready for oral hygiene. My life was really getting exciting now!

I flossed to Mary J. Blige's "All That I Can Say" and got to thinking about how the start of a song is so pure. Especially, the first time you hear those beginning bars because you *really* don't know where it's going to take you. It's one big, faithful surprise: power chords can turn into open ones, drums gain strength or patter lightly, a voice grows, envelopes notes, swims over the rhythm then mysteriously disappears.

Endings of songs, however, rarely have a commensurate spiritual effect. Instead, they're like a lot of things in life: just a lazy fade-out. All that energy at the jump turns into, like, whatever. I guess it must take too much effort to truly punctuate an ending and make it encompass all that's passed, round it all up, drive it out of the park.

If I played the lottery, the next day would have been a good day to pick numbers. Lucky Day Number Four. I found an $800 Hell's Kitchen studio sublet from a Swedish foreign exchange student named Cia (all decked out in IKEA, naturally) and a legit magazine connection.

My lit professor, Dr. Dowd, was the one who deserved all the credit for the latter.

"I was talking to an old Mizzou friend of mine about your big city adventure and he mentioned his sister-in-law works in magazine publishing in Manhattan."

"You're kidding." I crossed my legs while sitting on the windowsill, smoking a stale Dunhill I'd found under the TV set, winning the afternoon round of "FAC." There were some Spanish-speaking kids playing stickball on 52nd street. I coughed, but continued to puff away.

"Excuse me," I covered my mouth.

Dowd went on without interruption.

"Consider it payback for all the Byron research you did last semester. Let's see, she's at . . . " I could hear him riffling through papers and pictured the familiar lopsided piles on his messy desk, a spot infamous in the English Department. *"Boldly Beautiful."*

One jittery phone call later and I had an interview. That afternoon! I raced around the apartment getting dressed, which made my armpits perspire, so I sat down on the couch to do my makeup and review the subway map. Did the N-R connect to the B? How far did the L go? Would I make it on time?

I closed my eyes and visualized walking confidently into the *Boldly Beautiful* office and kicking ass at the interview. I tried not to think about screwing up what might be the biggest career opportunity of my life. I felt disheveled when I locked up Lucy's place, but I forced myself to face my destiny and walk forth into the sunlight.

By the time I made it to the offices of midtown, I felt like my whole body was quivering. I straightened out my posture and walked inside, stopping at the security desk to announce myself. They made a phone call and then gave me a sticky badge that read: 11. Nothing said professional like a sign reading, "Hello my name is . . . 11."

I whipped around to head to the elevators and came face-to-face with Derek Jeter. Yup, *the* Derek Jeter, who I found out later was gracing the cover of the men's lifestyle magazine in the building, so I hadn't completely imagined him. He let me go through the turnstile first. He made my knees wobble. I felt like the new kid on some Aaron Spelling show called *Magazine Assistant* and he was the special guest star. Yet something about him being from Kalamazoo, Michigan, gave me comfort in a very silly way and egged me onward.

Swing, batter, I told myself.

When I got to the hall, an elderly receptionist wearing bright red lipstick and a pink kerchief told me to have a seat. Minutes later a thirty-something, fashionably pregnant woman came out to greet me. I noticed her bright green mesh and sequined flowered slippers.

"Sophie," she came over to shake my hand. I stood and tried to wipe my palm on my thigh before taking her grasp.

"Come with me. We're going to meet the editor who needs a new assistant. Your boss-to-be." She put her arm around my shoulder and guided me through the glass door. I took a deep inhale.

“Her name is Claire Bonvay.”

“Pretty name,” I commented, lifting my head. Everything about the place seemed pretty, on the outside.

In one week, I’d landed a job and an apartment. Amazing that in such little time, my life had completely changed. Planets had aligned. I had wished for all of it, but it seemed to transform and unveil on its own. Equally miraculous was on Sunday of that week, I’d driven a giant U-Haul van straight through midtown Manhattan, and Lucy and I both lived to speak of it.

By Monday, I was beginning my career as an (already exhausted) official editorial assistant (that means I was senior to the mailroom guys, interns, and receptionists) at a real glossy magazine. In terms of “profile” and “top-shelf connections” it was a hot gig, no doubt. We were the ed assistants, the gritty worker bees out to prove ourselves for peanuts.

I got into a rhythm quickly. Each morning on my way walking to work, I’d clutch a cup of dirty coffee in my hand (same Athenos-themed paper cup at every donut stand), bypass Leona Helmsley’s hotel facing Park Avenue, and alternately hum Dolly Parton’s “9 to 5” and sing “I go to work, work, baby” in my smoothest and deepest Big Daddy Kane voice. It was really kind of romantic. And it seemed that in crazy NYC, being weird in public was like, the law, so I indulged. I sang loud.

I worked ten-hour days, and that sucked (forget about selling out my true feminist self by propagating nasty female stereotypes). “Gotta start somewhere and pay the rent” was my new urban mantra. In a sincere sense, I knew that I was damn lucky to be there and many recent grads would kill to be in my Daffy’s half-off Mary Janes.

I'd play music on my computer at work to keep myself entertained, pass the time and compose the soundtrack for my daydreaming about home and new, weird life—anything from Belle & Sebastian to Black Sabbath. Spinning the latter heavy metal group really annoyed the nasty male senior editor (with bad breath) who sat across the divide.

Secretly, this pleased me because nasty male editor (aka N.M.E.) would always make me run to the corner café in the afternoons to fetch him a soy latte with milk froth. No matter that I wasn't *his* assistant or that sometimes it was raining really hard, he'd demand me to go. Once he'd even made me return to the café because the foam's chi wasn't "happy enough." Prince of Fucking Darkness it was.

The pay was meager—$21,000 plus overtime—and the assignments of the "5 Signs He Likes You, 5 Signs He Doesn't" variety. I'd been haunted by questions like these all my life and now, go figure, here I was providing the answers!

Furthermore, "musical coverage" in celebrity sycophantic *Boldly Beautiful* regularly included Russell Crowe's band and the Bacon Brothers. Knowing that, let's just say I wasn't feeling particularly connected to the content.

At the close of my first month, the magazine was throwing its annual gala at Lincoln Center. I'd heard the cost of erecting the outdoor tents and putting on the lavish production was somewhere in the low millions.

The staff was spending even later nights churning out more content around the party and wrangling celebrities like Jewel, Jennifer Lopez, and Debra Messing to make appearances (there were a couple female politicians being honored too, but no one could remember their names). All the hoopla got even cynical *moi* excited about the affair so one afternoon near to the event, I asked my cubicle neighbor, May, what she was planning to wear.

"You do know that we don't get to go, right? Only a couple of the senior editors."

I wrinkled my face. A *Boldly Beautiful* party that the whole staff wasn't invited to? That didn't make any sense.

"Yeah, of course," I said sinking into my chair. It was hard to feel like we mattered much at that moment.

By month two, I was getting to my apartment so late each weeknight that by the time I shoved down a grilled cheese or veggie melt, I'd pass out on the couch in front of the TV and get up to do it all over again. The routine didn't bother me too much though because my social life wasn't exactly exploding and I was too poor for real fun.

Ironically, QVC was my favorite channel those nights. I think all those pleasant women with well-manicured nails and sparkly jewels made me feel like I wasn't all alone. It was like they were speaking right to me and we were comparing accessories. One susceptible evening, this extra-vanilla soccer mom type convinced me to buy a $150 knife set. I justified the extreme cost by telling myself they could pare avocados or stab an intruder.

Claire, my boss at *Boldly Beautiful,* was as pretty as her name: a chestnut brown-haired, holding-forty, native East Coaster who wore tortoiseshell glasses, loved Frat rock like the Dave Matthews Band and Barenaked Ladies, and flatly encouraged me to, and I quote, "engage in more office gossip." She tossed around SAT words like a college counselor, peppering her sentences with a couple of *fucks* and *shits* for dramatic effect. I'd already managed to discover a flask in her junk drawer, tucked underneath a copy of *The Seven Habits of Highly Effective People* and next to a wholesale-sized pack of Tic Tacs.

Hands down, the worst part of the gig was lunch. Our extravagant $30 million cafeteria was designed by Vont$, a chichi, Dutch uber-architect; this fact, I'll admit, was alluring since back in eleventh grade art history class I'd written a twelve-page report on one of his architectural masterpieces in southern Spain. But, it also seemed like a whole lotta money to squander on an eatery where many of your employees just masticated mesclun with a dollop of balsamic vinegar and dribble of olive oil.

(I also felt kind of disgusted at the gargantuan price tag when thinking about how that fancy café money could have fed an entire population of poor, starving children in some Third World Nation!)

Personally speaking, perhaps it too was that this employee took eating seriously and had to stand uncomfortably in line with the leafy-green girls while she paid for her carb-loving meal option of pasta, frites, and dessert. Forget fro-yo honey, I was all over that bomb chocolate cake. And, I had virtually no competition getting to it (a nice aside). I just got a lot of evil looks from self-deprived females.

Another example of modern couture torture: Even when you and your wobbly tray would attempt an elegant exit in a new Club Monaco skirt (splurge), everyone in the room (80 percent women under 34) seated in the bulbous, see-through booths shaped like giant seashells would be glaring at your sale shoes and stride.

That's when you might trip a little because you were slightly nervous and God had mistakenly given you size ten feet to go with your petite frame. It was too stressful. Worse than middle school 'cause now, I swear, everyone was at a popular table.

If that wasn't bad enough, *Boldly Beautiful* was on the eleventh floor, which meant we had to take the elevators with the girls who worked at the most chic, snotty fashion magazine in our midtown building. One day, I forced my way into one of those closing elevators, and found myself riding alone (instrumental Nirvana's "Smells Like Teen Spirit" playing softly in the chamber), with the mega-thin, Chanel-suited, editor-in-chief of said fashion tome who looked me up as I got inside. *Yeah, screw you too,* I thought.

I was sure she was glaring at me behind my back and no doubt sizing up my, shall we say, *very* casual Friday wardrobe. In fact, I could hear her panting behind me. I spent those eleven floors knocking my New Balances against the door, feeling like a complete fashion failure and chanting "open" in my head.

When I got back to the office and dished to Claire that I'd just ridden with Madame Mauvais, she started laughing hysterically.

"Sophie sweetie, don't you know you're supposed to let her ride alone? It's an unspoken company policy."

I felt so dumb but I tried to hide it.

"Well, nobody told me," I said in a huff. "It's not like it was fun or anything." I shrugged. "She's like the wicked witch of Oz in a three-thousand-dollar outfit. Creepy vibes."

After a few months of writing relationship and STD stories and dealing with daily coworker mini-drama, I was starting to crash—*hard.* I skipped lunches all together and just stood outside and chain-smoked Marlboro Lights. I no longer cared if my boss saw me surfing music websites, got downright sick of answering the phone with a fake, perky voice and started coming in late. Even annoying the halitosis male editor with Minor Threat's "Best Of" wasn't fun anymore.

Understandably, my boss was concerned. I wasn't exactly the most go-get-'em assistant. One night, we'd had a one-on-one meeting about how to be "boldly beautiful *and* beautifully bold." But the office rumors, the cattiness, and the useless subject matter had already started to steal my soul. I was parading my discontent all over the building and even if I'd wanted to hold back, it seemed I couldn't restrain myself. We'd already reached the crescendo of this one.

I liked and respected many of my coworkers, but really wished to work in a more diverse, loose atmosphere where I was one of the many ethnic staffers; where being creative was encouraged, not squashed; where Gwyneth Paltrow's mating habits didn't rule; and where hetero guys roamed around. Preferably naked, but really at that point, I'd take anything.

Just a place where people were relaxed enough to make eye contact with you in the hallway.

My *Boldly Beautiful* reign would drag on for a few more months, but something gave me hope that there were greener pastures ahead.

One night after I'd left the office, a kid in an orange fleece and Timberland backpack handed me a red flyer for a hip-hop Open Mic Night on the Bowery. So that following Sunday evening, I went to the spot alone, paid my five bones at the door, and sat in the back where kids were busting open cigars and filling up the insides with buds. They were leaning on one another, puffing away and nodding their heads in rhythm to the emcees on the stage.

Then, in between sets, this handsome light-skinned boy with broad shoulders, milk chocolate eyes, and a Mixwell shirt gently asked me my name and whether or not I'd ever been to the joint before. I shook my head no and then he put his hand out and introduced himself as "Furious."

I asked him whether he got his name from the father in *Boyz in the Hood* and he said, "Well . . . kinda," looked away and smiled. At the end of the night, he asked for my digits and I passed him my pink business card.

"You work for *Boldly Beautiful* magazine?" he said, raising an eyebrow.

I cocked my hip and croaked, "yes."

"And you like rap?" he asked skeptically, tilting his head.

"That's why I came," I answered and walked away.

A few days later, the phone at work rang and I put my headset on to answer it.

"*Boldly Beautiful,* this is Sophie."

"Yo, boldly beautiful Sophie, why'd you run away from me the other night?"

I was hoping Furious would call me and I smiled. He seemed devilish but not dirty. The epitome of Fun.

"So, what's your real name, anyway?" I asked twirling the phone cord and crossing my legs.

"If I told you, I'd have to kill you," he said.

We waited in a hush.

"Lame," I sighed.

"But I got something else for you to dig on now: an album release party for my boys P.A.K. at the Academy of Music. You know where that is?"

"Sort of," I said.

"It's just off the C train in Fort Greene. Lafayette stop."

"Okay, that helps."

"It's tonight and I already put you on the list. Bring a friend, if you want to," he urged.

His assertiveness was mighty attractive.

"Thanks," I said.

"A platonic friend," he added.

"Ha."

"Just come, I wanna see your face again, baby."

"Okay," I said, tapping a pen against the phone. "I'll try."

I copied down the address and speed dialed the four-digit extension to Sam, my friend in photo. He was gay, wore Hugo Boss suits almost every day, and sat opposite me in the far corner of our office.

I convinced him to party with me in record time and all it cost me was his cocktail drink tab.

"I'll just borrow something to wear from the Fashion Closet."

Sam loved any excuse to break into that thing and have his way with the designer clothes on loan. I couldn't believe I was taking him to a hip-hop party; but my mag-girl/music-whore duality was nascent, and I wanted others to cross over with me.

I hurried home after work to change for the party. I didn't know what to wear! This was my first hip-hop party so I wanted to look tasteful and sultry and definitely not alternative. That wouldn't fly. I flung clothes from my closet onto my bed and changed the CD four times from Nas to Patsy Cline to Destiny's Child to Johnny Cash.

I felt anxious, like at the start of the school year. Well, at least my toes looked good, I thought—the palest pink you could imagine, just a smidge subtler than cotton candy. However, I couldn't very well divert folks' attention to my delightful twelve-dollar pedicure all night.

Sam rang the doorbell; I was still in a towel. He shook his head in disappointment.

"Is that what you're wearing? Do not try to out-slut me, Sophie." He pushed open the door and went straight for my bedroom.

I watched him thumb through the clothes, slide the hangers back and forth, shake his head, make tsk-tsk noises. He turned to face me.

"How about this?"

I waited a moment to decide.

"Ummmm," I pondered.

"Actually no," he said. "You're wearing it. The End."

He forced me into a denim pencil skirt and an asymmetrical pastel orange top. We stood in front of my full-length mirror; a twenty-first birthday present from Mom who wanted me to appreciate my "youthful figure" from head to toe before it slipped away to aging.

As I looked at myself, I felt more discomfort than admiration. My long, thick hair that I clipped into a ponytail was now frizzing in rebellion; my smoky-eyes makeup application that I'd followed from my new Kevyn Aucoin book was making my already big browns frog-sized; and my legs, though tanned and athletic, had two bruises on the shins where I'd bumped into my coffee table. Twice. In a row.

"You have nice shoulders," Sam said, as though he could intuit my insecurities. He placed his warm hands on them and I noticed he was kind of right. He freed my hair and it fell all around me. "You're exotic."

"But I never look totally put together," I whined, yanking on my skirt and turning to the side.

"Looking 'totally put together,'" he finger-quoted, "is for the bridge-and-tunnel crowd. Now, let's make like Tom and cruise."

"Okay," I chuckled, heading with him down the narrow hallway to the door. "And may I say that you are looking mighty handsome yourself in that blazer."

"Yes, you may and *merci beaucoup*," he said and reached for the knob. For some reason, he liked expressing gratitude in different languages. I loved this man.

When we got to the party, Sam said that it was largest group of hetero men he'd seen in one place since his U-Dub days. I thought, *score*. Then he added, "Largest group of undatable hetero men." Maybe he'd had a premonition.

"So, where's *the* guy?" he asked, tipping back his vodka gimlet.

"Sam, I don't even know if I even like him. He just seemed cool, different."

"Yeah, sure, whatever. So where is he?" Sam asked fanning a puff of smoke away. It looked like a mushroom cloud had set in the middle of the barely lit club. I felt a barrage of shoulders rub on by. I worried about my poor, helpless toes vulnerably exposed in my thong heels. In this hectic scene, I could have used my trusty old steel-tipped Doc Martins.

"Furious," I said, rubbing my nose and fearing an acute allergy attack.

"What?"

"That's his name."

"Are you serious?"

I smiled and he let out a diva laugh.

"That's hysterical!"

We found out that P.A.K. was an underground, politically charged rap group from Bed-Stuy, a rough, predominantly black neighborhood in the middle of Brooklyn. At least, that's what the flyer I picked up read. It almost seemed that the actual group, the reason for the event, was an afterthought to the reverie at hand: a rectangular, hazy club with sticky wood floors and purple neon lights. A Hispanic-looking deejay at the end of the room, set a bit higher than the rest of us and myriad youngish, mostly minority people, in pageboy caps, slouchy dark denim fits, short leather skirts and high to the sky heels kissing hello or really getting to know one another by grinding on the dance floor.

It was almost an impenetrable mass of movement and tan people and smiles and cognac glasses and cigars, with a whole lot of bass bumping in the background.

Sam and I popped a squat in a tiny corner by a big window where we vowed not to bitch about work all night and, instead, started a drinking game where we counted Ché Guevara shirts. The chronic in the air smelled like one giant, ripe armpit. I spotted three tees through the fog, beating Sam by one. We moved to the bar to even up. Or at least we tried to move by pushing past all the sweaty bodies, eyeing the bottles on the horizon, and repeating "excuse me" about a hundred times.

"This is a cool scene, don't you think?" I said, once we'd retreated to a safe, vacant, six-inch corner of the bar by the olives and oranges wedges. "And this album sounds good, kind of like old De La but grimier."

"Thank you, Tabitha Soren," he said, flipping his hair.

I cracked up, nodding my head to the rhythm. It was fun to see Sam out of his element—me too. I finally spotted Furious at the doorway, dressed in his urban-prep best. He noticed me, waved and came our way. People in the club were now rapping along to Special Ed as the deejay sidelined P.A.K. and entered an Old Skool set.

"Nice getup," I said smiling. And I meant it: a brown Izod shirt, flat front khakis and black wallabies.

"Yeah, is it a 'Do'?" he grinned, smoothing down the button-up over his torso.

I laughed and nodded.

"I thought I'd clean up a bit," he smiled back and outstretched his arms.

"This is my friend from work, Sam," I presented him as though he were a prize.

They shook hands.

"Sorry I'm so late. I was out recording. Are y'all having a good time?"

I looked at Sam who nodded politely and polished off another cocktail.

"Smashing time," Sam said, smiling wide. Sometimes he reminded me of a fey Hugh Grant.

"Cool, dude," Furious replied. "There's someone I wanted you to meet, Sophie," he said placing his hand my shoulder. "This cat from *BeatMaker*. He's the photo editor or some shit. He just shot me for a feature story. You know that magazine?"

"Oh yeah," I said, nodding. "I've read it off and on for, like, ever. You're gonna be in it?"

He popped his collar.

"I'm gonna be large, babe. A star. It's a done deal," he smiled. "Anyway, he told me they're looking for an editor, so I said I knew the perfect lady. You interested?"

"Yeah, I am."

He patted the small of my back.

"I'll go find him," he said and walked away.

I met Amon a few minutes later. He was tall, East Indian–looking, and a word mumbler, which made our meeting even more challenging and stressful. Sam hovered somewhat uncomfortably as the third wheel and occupied himself by playing with the ice in his glass while we schmoozed. After the intro pleasantries, Furious went ghost and me and Amon's banter swiftly and inevitably turned to music.

"So do you just bump hip-hop?" Amon asked.

I shook my head.

"Nope. My tastes are all over the place. I listen to everything from blues to soul, rock to punk, everything except possibly . . . and I'm sort of embarrassed to admit this to you . . . "

He smiled.

"Go on."

"Funk."

"Awwwww," he said, tossing his head back. "You're missing out."

"I know, I know. It's bad," I said, waving him off.

"Pardonnez-moi," Sam said, dipping his head over my shoulder. "But I'm going for another round. You want?"

"I'm all right, thanks," I said, rubbing his cheek.

Amon shook his head.

"I'm not drinkin', but thanks anyway, man."

Sam took off into the dark abyss. The deejay was back to playing P.A.K., and a crew of breakers took over the dance floor.

"Are you straight-edge or something?" I asked Amon, half-joking.

"Nah, I'm just hungover from last night, but—"

He pulled up the sleeve of his Independent hoodie and revealed a giant, black X tattooed on his wrist.

"I was. Back in high school when it was cool."

"I was gonna say. Seeing your tattoo sure does bring back the teenage memories," I said. "Me and my best friend snapping pictures of cute skaters downtown for hours on end until it was time for Veggie Whoppers at the local BK."

He laughed.

"That brings back memories too," he said, pointing to the dance floor where the breakers had put down some cardboard and were taking turns dancing on it.

"Ah, the eighties," I reflected.

Amon smiled.

"You're probably too young to remember them."

"Actually no," I said. "But they're coming back anyway, right?"

"Oh yeah. New Wave, all that. You a fan?"

I dipped into my mental music catalog.

"In this order: The Church, The Cure, Joy Division."

"Dark yet romantic," he commented.

"Yeah, I was angst-ridden. Typical." I shrugged.

"I freaking love Joy Division." He ran his fingers through his straight, black, moptop hair.

"Okay, well how about this: Furious told me *BeatMaker* might be looking for an editor, so how about we trade cards, you agree to pass my résumé along to your HR department and I'll hook you up with the sweetest, most obscure MP3 version of 'Love Will Tear Us Apart' you've ever heard."

"It's a deal," he smiled. We shook hands.

Amen for Amon. I felt like he was a human turning point. He put my card in his wallet and gave me a kiss on the cheek.

"Cool talking to you. We'll catch up soon," he said and exited the party.

While waiting for Sam to return, I leaned on a wall and scanned the crowd. The party had thinned out some. I spotted Furious on the dance floor, cozying up to a cute, petite Asian girl dressed all in Baby Phat. Minutes later, he was doing the wop with another chick to Wu-Tang.

Sam came back empty-handed and weathered from the rowdy scene at the bar, so we decided to split. I didn't say bye to Furious, who seemed occupied with the little lady #1, but the next day, as promised, I e-mailed Amon the MP3, my résumé, and a cover letter detailing my great need to be a contributor to the magazine. I tossed in a check for a million bucks with my clips, made out to "Amon's the Mon," which I think was charming (or pitiful) enough to keep my package moving up the masthead.

A week later, their managing editor, Dana, called me into the offices for an interview. I found out that she was from Grosse Pointe, went to Northwestern, and was trying to beef up the music magazine with more female editors. She seemed impressed that I worked for *Boldly Beautiful* "at such a young age," liked that I was from the midwest and "diverse in musical taste." (But, we really bonded over our secret passion for *NSYNC.)

Luck in work had rained down once more, assuring me, in a sense, that NYC was the right place to do this. Or, at least, keep going. The M.E. said she'd get back to me in few weeks so I held on, waiting for the call, playing *No Strings Attached* to pass the time and foster positive vibes.

About seven working days later, an assistant, Charlotte, called me to say the M.E. was giving me a trial interview, but not with an editor, with a rapper. Charlotte asked if I'd be cool with that so she could go ahead and organize it.

For some reason, I pictured a dirty, snaggletooth Project Pat in my head and he was waving me with one finger into his Bentley.

I tried to not sound nervous or reluctant when I agreed but a very real doubt was creeping up my body. Who the hell did I think I was? These guys would see right through me. Gobble me up. I loved music, I'd listened and appreciated rap for years, but I didn't know everything about it, every fact or important album. I was still learning. And, at the moment, dressed in my black cigarette pants and Filth Mart cut-up Led Zeppelin T-shirt, I sure didn't look like I repped it, either. Fuck me!

"Great," Charlotte said. "I'll set it up and holler at you with all the details."

"That's word, thanks." I swallowed. My slang sounded so

fabricated, even though I'd grown up speaking it. "Sounds good," I gentrified.

"Talk to you soon," she said with a click.

I sat at my desk with the phone still at my ear. I was frozen in the same moment I'd experienced when I was twelve visiting Cedar Point with my seventh-grade class and my crush, Mike De-Carte, persuaded me onto my first roller coaster. On the psychotic Magnum ride, I remember looking over at Mike whose limbs were flailing in the air and realizing how boys could make me do stupid things. Thrilling and scary things I'd never considered before.

Music, like men, was potent in usurping my better judgment. I was a kid in The Pied Piper, unable to resist its seductive calling and completely clueless as to what challenges lay ahead on the path.

dolo

I was counting the minutes until Charlotte called again. The next days at *Boldly Beautiful* continued being really regular and excruciatingly slow. Same tummy flip-flops when the schizophrenic ed-in-chief barked my name and criticized my writing, then dialed my extension from across the newsroom to tell me "job well done" on one of those just-harped-on ideas. Mister stinky breath editor wouldn't stop humming Natalie Imbruglia's "Torn" and praising Kylie Minogue as "fab."

Furthermore, I'd come vis-à-vis with what I deemed a troubling "hyphenate habit," whereby all my writing now included lots of spice-you-up looks, get-me-out-of-there miracles, what-brought-us-back-together tales, bring-out-the-best-in-you trends. Our senior editors were get-me-to-the-mental-ward cuckoo for this pesky, yet alarmingly addictive, sorority girl phrasing. I could feel myself getting dumber and more inarticulate by the minute.

Claire was PMS-ing and kept her office door shut all day while sending me curt e-mails through the glass about her needs (mainly Funyons and Kit Kats) and my duties (mostly staying out of her way). I filed contracts, restocked our stationery, talked with the mailroom boy about hip-hop (he was from the Bronx and loved the Cash Money clique), and pitched more ideas on how to get a guy to fall in love with you. Meanwhile, it seemed that the real problem was getting him (and you) to stay there.

One ongoing image repeatedly flashed in front of me: sitting at that cold, white desk under that nasty fluorescent light for the next twenty years of my life, editing copy about Botox, picking at stress zits on my chin while the Research Department down the hall tortured me with the Dido album. A lot was riding on *BeatMaker*.

Friday of that week, while I was e-mailing Lucy and finalizing weekend plans, the strangest, most Doors-ian, unexpected, trippy thing happened: My boss called me into her office, sat me down in the corner and said,

"Sophie, you've been fired."

I let out a laugh. She didn't.

"You're joking, right?" I squeaked.

I watched in horror her head wave from side-to-side.

"Fired?" My mouth filled with sand.

Claire, glassy-eyed, launched into some sort of speech but all I heard was wah-wah-wah-fired. She couldn't face me directly though, so technically she addressed the oration to my shoulder, but I caught the gist of it: pink-slipped. Don't let the door hit you on the way out.

"Why?" was an even harder question for her to answer but she tried.

I can't fully remember the entire load of bunk she spewed as I zoned out from the pain, but in essence she pointed the finger at *Boldly Beautiful*'s multiple personality disorder E-I-C who was experiencing some serious mood swings and seemed to have canned me for sport. Shit, I hadn't even known she really knew my name.

"I'm sorry, Sophie. You know our E-I-C can be really erratic. Consider yourself part of a honorable club of editors she's let go. There are a lot of them," Claire said, in a flawed attempt to comfort me.

"Honorable?" I hmmphed.

"Maybe I could have fought harder for you. I'm sorry about that part," she continued.

"Were you even happy with my work?"

She nodded.

"I mean, I *tried*." I wanted to defend myself harder, but I felt so weak. Crushed like a can under life's heel.

"Maybe it's for the better," Claire said. "Maybe your dream isn't to work at a women's magazine forever."

I bit my lip and tried to hold back from crying in Claire's presence.

"I guess you're right about that," I conceded. Fuck it.

I was a goner. Eighty-sixed. Out of there. One month's notice to polish off my pieces and find a new gig. The more I told myself, the less real it seemed.

"A lot of top editors liked my writing," I said, on my way out of her office.

Claire frowned.

"Yes," she whispered. "We're going to miss you."

I went home, unplugged the phone, gulped a six-pack of Coors

Light keg cans and smoked straight through a box of Camel Wides while playing Elliott Smith's *XO*. Rejection. Self-pity. Exorcizing the hurt. Dulling the senses. In the eternal, controversial words of The Judybats, pain makes you beautiful. Or just makes me into a basket case.

Take my word, trying to mount my whirling bed later that night, after already tumbling off the side once, was neither beautiful nor gracious. Possibly comical, but I was too close to my own misery to laugh.

I'd also bawled so hard that when I sobered up and awoke in the middle of the night, I'd gotten a stuffy nose and a migraine. I learned that getting fired sucked, even when you didn't like your job. Which I felt was truly unfair. Please don't say it. That's the worst motto of all time. It makes a mockery out of despair.

I felt like a giant failure so I decided not to tell any of my coworkers I was out until my very last day. That way, no questions and even better, no need for holey explanations.

I managed a sloppy, stuttering but sincere prayer asking God to help me be strong and to get the *BeatMaker* job. I bartered "no curse words." Or at least I think I did cause my phone rang the next Monday morning and I felt extra guilty saying the F-word. It was the Michigan M.E. coming to save me, horseless and hopeful. My trial assignment: tomorrow, Ja Rule, on camera at Def Jam's offices in midtown.

"Charlotte will e-mail you more of the details. We're on a deadline so I can't chat, but good luck," she said and hung up before I chirped, "thanks. Bye."

I had never been to Def Jam before or any other record label for that matter. But, I had heard the legendary tale of Russell Simmons and Rick Rubin starting the company in an NYU dorm room overlooking Washington Square Park and busting out with Public Enemy and the Beastie Boys and Run-DMC and how their college dream, probably no bigger than my own, had parlayed itself into a multimillion dollar empire now headed by Lyor Cohen, a tough, shrewd CEO with transparent, stern blue eyes.

Or, at least, that's how his peepers looked on TV. Don't ask me why I imagined he'd be holding the doors like Hades at the Gates of Def Jam Hell, sizing people up, but I did. At that beginning point in my career, nobody gave a shit about me, or my green opinions (especially as a girl). I was completely naïve to this and really that was better—even in hindsight—because it made me very serious, opinionated and on guard. I wanted to show people that I was different, but that I could still belong. I wanted to respect and be respected.

demo

In the morning of my interview, I awoke at 6:30 a.m. I stayed in my PJs, centered myself with deep breaths and tried to prepare for the challenge. I wanted to appear important and qualified and in control.

I mostly accomplished this by reading about ten recent Ja Rule interviews, by downing four cups of coffee, and superficially by ironing my carefully chosen clothes and laying out the finale on my bed: open-toe black pumps, A-line army green skirt, three-quarter-sleeved, black button-up top, and big-ass gold hoops.

Frankly, Ja Rule's image scared me a bit. While I'd enjoyed a couple drunken dances to "Holla, Holla" up in the club, I hadn't been a big diehard fan or anything. Besides, this was about a month before *Rule 3:36* dropped, so he wasn't extremely popular with the mainstream yet. I'd read in a couple places he'd given Jay-Z the beat for "Can I Get A" and that was one of the things he was most famous for. Plus, what a classic song! Also, he'd had a rough, street-raised childhood and his new song "Thing That You Do" was jiggy and flirty and gaining airplay fast. These were the facts I had to go on.

The interview could go anywhere. I didn't care, I just prayed, "Please, Lord, let it go *some*where." I needed to make the man talk. I'd just be myself and try to engage him in a conversation. No biggie, right?

The one sure thing I did have going for me was that celebrity status didn't intimidate me. Whenever I'd start to feel nervous or in awe about a famous person, I'd remember that they poop in the toilet too and that'd abolish any of those exceptional thoughts.

I called in sick to *Boldly Beautiful* (not that Claire cared anymore) and right up to my twelve o'clock appointment contemplated canceling on Ja. Since I didn't even know who to call for this, I had no choice but to go.

The Def Jam offices are set in the center of a whole block, so I had to twirl around the curvy building in a couple circles before I actually found the right door. This was highly embarrassing since I imagined Mr. Cohen peering down from some window at me having a hearty laugh, but I still tried to act like I knew where I was going. I tried to walk with purpose; New Yorkers are incredibly deft at creating this illusion.

The camera guy, Shawn, was standing inside and I was like three minutes late, so I apologized about five times. He seemed nice and he kept fumbling with the mic in the elevator, flipping it off and on and testing it, so his nervousness made me calmer.

"I don't work full-time for *BeatMaker,*" he said once we'd cleared security and were in the elevator. "I just freelance when they need me. Amon is my roommate."

"Oh," I said. "I know him."

He nodded.

"Where else do you work?" I asked.

"I got a part-time gig at *The Howard Stern Show*."

"So what's crazier, Howard Stern or the hip-hop world?" I asked.

He thought about it for a moment.

"Tough question. Hip-hop definitely."

"Great. Now I know what I'm in for."

We laughed.

"You'll be fine," he said.

I wanted to believe him.

The doors opened, we introduced ourselves to the receptionist and a frenzied, tall, Latina publicist dressed in a baggy Roc-A-Fella jumpsuit and Gucci fannypack came out the corridor to fetch us. The offices looked like *Boldly Beautiful,* just with many more hip young guys engrossed in reading their computer screens, stacks of CDs everywhere and a serious amount of urban music posters on the walls.

She led us into a conference room where a compact, muscular black guy sat in a white T-shirt and black bandanna with his back to the door, hunched over a magazine, smoke wafting from a gigantic blunt lying in an ashtray next to his hand. There was a young, shy dishwater blond girl sitting quietly in the corner. I sighed and almost turned right around but momentum moved me ahead.

"Ja, this is Sophie. She's from *BeatMaker*." He didn't even look up from the magazine, which I was now close enough to recognize as *The Source*. She repeated my stellar intro. He slowly turned up from the magazine and, at first, looked thoroughly bothered by my presence but then broke a smile.

"Hey," I said. He was cuter in person. Compact.

"When can I eat?" he said looking up at the publicist.

"Just *BeatMaker* and then you get a break. Promise."

He rolled his eyes.

I wondered why he had to wait to eat lunch. Didn't they feed the rappers? Now I had an irritable, starving person on my hands. Lordy.

I took a seat next to him. He was still looking at the magazine, puffing on the blunt. I waited uncomfortably while Shawn fumbled with the camera. Ja's probably sizing me up as some prissy suburbs girl, I thought. Some old-school Vanilla Ice fan.

"Ready," he said focusing on me and Ja Rule.

"How about you and I just face each other and Shawn can maybe shoot over my shoulder. What do you think?" I asked.

Ja shrugged and Shawn agreed.

Here goes nothing, I thought. Safety bar locked. Ja looked like he was about to fall asleep.

I was always interested in how musicians got their start in their art so this was my first question.

"When did you start rhyming?"

He slowly came to life.

"I don't know if there was a start. I was just always writing. Growing up in Hollis, that's what all the kids were into."

He went on to talk about working with Jay-Z and making beats, producing, his clique, Murder Inc.

"Me and the whole Murder Inc. fam rented a huge house in Cali to record the new joint. It was off the chain. Crazy bananas for two months straight. Bullshit and party and write music. Dream come true, man."

"I can imagine," I said. "Something like a hip-hop frat house?"

"Yeah, but worse," he laughed.

"Did it make a difference recording on the West Coast versus the East?"

"It was more fun to make the record, more at ease. So the songs aren't all as heavy."

"I could hear that," I said. "Like your new single."

"Exactly. It's got a lighter feel to it."

We talked about a couple of new acting roles. He said he couldn't rap forever. I brought up the topic of his kids. Immediately, I noticed a change: it was as if someone had plugged him into an electrical socket. He put his feet on his chair, smiled wide, started waving his hands around. Like any other proud parent, I supposed.

I asked him if he thought he was a good father.

"I love my kids and they know that. So I try to be," he nodded.

I waited.

"You see," he said. "I don't really know what a good father is because . . . I never had one. But, I think I am. I hope so."

His statement made a big impact. I was impressed with his self-deconstruction. I also felt bad for the guy.

"Okay, so let me ask you this . . . " We were both leaning into each other now. I'd even forgotten Shawn was taping us. Ja took a drag off the blunt.

"If you could teach your kids one lesson, what would it be?"

He paused, holding in the smoke, grinned, looked me in the eye and directly into the camera lens.

"Don't do drugs." The haze billowed out of his mouth.

We all fell out laughing! Ja was laughing and coughing and laughing and coughing. It was too funny.

Man, he'd won me over. He was a charmer and you could see that twinkle in his eye. He was going to be huge. Next level.

We finally all gained our composure.

"But I'm serious," he said firmly. "That's what I would want them to learn."

"Cool," I nodded. It felt like we were friends or something. After the interview ended, I wished him well with the album.

"Thanks," he said, shaking my hand.

The publicist met me in the hallway and told me I could get on the list for the rapper's show on Friday.

"I can probably get you a plus one, if you want."

I pondered this question without knowing what "plus one" truly meant. But then I figured it out.

"Nope, it's just me." I answered. Even though I knew I'd probably flake and just watch QVC all night.

We shook hands and split.

Shawn and I scored an elevator and I told him that I was on the biggest high.

"Maybe it's a contact buzz," he said laughing.

"Maybe," I nodded. "But I don't think that's wholly responsible. That was just a hell of a lot of fun. I mean, when we first got in the room, I was pretty sure the guy was like, over me from the get. But he really opened up." I sighed. "He was hilarious too. And nice." I could not shut up. It felt like I had a new crush.

"Yeah, you were good."

"I was? Thanks," I said, taking an exaggerated breath.

"I was thinking when I turned on the camera, 'She might have a rough time with this,' but you really pulled it off."

What a rush! Until Shawn and I hit the outdoors and he wished me good luck with *BeatMaker* and I realized that's right, I don't officially have the job yet.

"Are you walking to the train?"

"Yeah, but I think I might have a smoke first. Chill out."

"Cool," he said putting his camera bag over his shoulder. "Maybe I'll see you around." We shook hands.

"Hope so," I said, waving. "Say hi to Amon."

He looked over his shoulder and nodded.

I stood there, mesmerized.

Suddenly, a swarm of black kids came over and one passed me a cassette tape, snapping me back to the present tense.

"What is it?" I asked.

"It's us. We're called First Down."

"Okay . . . " I was still confused.

"Maybe you can give it to one of your A&R peeps?"

"Oh." Lights on. "Unfortunately, I don't work here."

"You sure?"

"Pretty sure, yeah." I smiled.

"Okay, okay," he shot back. His friends hovered about, looking on.

"I'm sorry I'm not the right person," I said feeling like a disappointment. He was silent. I shook my head. "Want it back?" I asked, holding the tape out.

"It's aight, keep it," he said. "You look important." He winked.

"Oh yeah? Thanks." I stuffed it into my coat pocket like he had.

"Easy," he said, walking away with his crew.

"Good luck," I smiled.

I took a couple more drags of my smoke. Within minutes, another young Puerto Rican–looking kid with a navy headband and Yankees jacket started walking toward me with his hand in his pocket. Didn't anybody go to school anymore?

"Sorry. I don't work here," I said at the risk of being presumptuous.

He nodded and kept walking. I found standing there too strange so I stubbed out my cigarette and headed for the train while daydreaming about Ja. I was alone, but it didn't matter right then. I was satisfied enough with myself that I didn't have to tell anyone. I even patted myself on the back. (That geeky move I definitely wouldn't be telling anyone.)

That following day I had to return and face my fate at *Boldly Beautiful,* but my little secret . . . my miniature coup, so delicately merciful, gave me just enough courage and restored just enough dignity that as I heaved open the dense chrome doors to that magazine monstrosity, I almost felt, well . . . stronger.

how to catch feelings

Boldly Beautiful was busy sapping me of all my creativity, and my last day was looming in the not so distant future. *BeatMaker,* on the other hand, was busy keeping me on hold, giving me a hard copy edit test and, probably, an ulcer from all the anticipation. I decided to do what any young single girl would: party my booty off in a concerted effort to balance my work stress with hard play.

The sweltering, sticky summer of 1999 was in full swing, and soulful songbird/emcee Lauryn Hill had recently stepped out solo to reveal a whole album detailing her own complicated experience of female love: that one-woman adventure ship undulating in turbid water.

Sometimes her words on *The Miseducation . . .* were so raw and her voice so fragile and intimate that I actually got embarrassed simply from listening. She was about my age when she wrote that album; articulating many of the feelings I couldn't understand, but now plagued me.

During that maddeningly hot season in New York, you could hear "Doo Wop (That Thing)" and "Ex Factor" and "Can't Take My Eyes off of You" from Flatbush to Washington Heights, Grand Concourse to Bay Ridge. The vulnerability of her lyrics, blended with her musical passion, was the most seductive summer cocktail I'd tasted in recent memory.

The fact that her private offering was made so public—bursting from cars and windows across the island and down the shores—only added to its mysterious effect. It was a heart takeover. And I was a Lauryn believer, marching faithfully by her side.

Then that play-hard Friday night at the end of July, I got shoved to the front lines. Lucy, who I hadn't seen in three weeks; her two new uptown friends she'd met at downtown Jivamukti Yoga, Justine and Julia; and I all piled into a taxi and headed unawares to a rent party in Brooklyn. It was being thrown by one of Julia's old classmates from SVA. I teased Lucy and asked her if she wanted to bring her yoga mat with, but she declined and didn't laugh.

"Nothing Even Matters" was playing softly with a side of static in the cab as we crossed the Williamsburg Bridge. The driver reeked of wet socks, and the Zen chicks in the backseat were already buzzed and giggling incessantly like giddy cheerleaders. Must be all that standing on your head, I thought.

I hummed along to the faint music, craning my neck to watch the grand and elegant Manhattan skyline receding; thinking about the way Ryan stroked my collarbone when he kissed me. Missing the security of his embrace, the sincerity of his affection, the stability and steadfastness of his being around, cracking up at my dumb jokes, forgiving me when I met him late for dinner, knowing my past failures. I felt very far away though, like that wonderfully depressing Harry Connick Jr. song about a lover set adrift.

Ryan was uncomplicated, real and more than I deserved. Now, I was surrounded by people who didn't get me at all, who regularly referred to things like "downward dog," and who obsessively, competitively brunched on Sunday like chipmunks storing acorns for the harried week. (My acorn of choice remained the provincial Cap'n Crunch cereal.)

When I stepped outside of the cab on Berry Street, the sky popped and crackled and I felt a cool raindrop plop down on my wrist. The graffiti tagged door to the apartment looked like an entrance to an abandoned building, which, I found out later, it mostly was. Just like the many other renovated old sweatshops that'd recently been taken over in the area by young artistes in need of space for stretching canvases and such, banging drums, spinning wheels, art du jour.

The trio followed and we all filed inside. Not long after our anticlimactic entrance, I had gravitated to the skill-less deejay busy spinning Prodigy's "Smack My Bitch Up" and "Firestarter" back-to-back, which, on top of being horrible music, was also seriously uncalled for since the party was still sparse and hadn't even caught a vibe yet.

So, there I was eyeing the turntables and trying to convince him to play an all-time crowd favorite, Pete Rock and CL Smooth's gem "They Reminisce over You," when a tall, suggestively muscular, disheveled, olive-skinned boy swaggered over and stood next to me, flipping through records. He turned and smiled my way, so I said *hey*. He was wearing a beat-up Black Sheep T-shirt, cargos, and red wristband. I think it took about twenty seconds for me to fall in love with him. My mystery boy's name was Jack Moretti.

"Do you like this song?" I asked, concentrating on his light green eyes, his stubble and his electric smile. "I requested it," I said, instantly racking up cool points.

"Yeah, it's a classic. I love the trombone chorus." He wiggled his long, spider-leg fingers in front of his mouth, playing a phantom brass.

"Soulful," I nodded.

"What are you, a deejay or something?"

I laughed.

"Uh, yeah. That's right. DJ Sophie." I put out my palm.

"Nice to meet you," he said, shaking it.

Just then a bald guy ran up behind Jack, knocking him to the side. Jack swatted the guy on his head. I cowered.

"This is my friend Noah."

I returned, cautious of the duo. Noah and I shook hands.

"This is DJ Sophie."

I smiled, teeth and all.

"What kind of deejay are you?" Noah asked.

"Hip-hop," I said, without thinking.

Noah nodded.

"I work at a hip-hop studio, Landmark. You should stop by sometime."

Jack shot Noah a scary look.

"Don't flirt with her," Jack said, yanking Noah away from me. I thought Jack was going to laugh but he didn't and Noah stepped back, wearing a mischievous mug.

I sensed some old rivalry unfolding before me. Lucy came around and peered over Jack's shoulder.

"We're leaving in ten minutes, Sophie."

"Don't you mean DJ Sophie?" Jack joshed.

Lucy's face scrunched up.

"Yeah, sure. *DJ* Sophie. Be outside in ten." She held up all ten fingers. Business.

I nodded and Lucy and Noah both jetted.

"See you around, Sophie," Noah said from a distance.

I waved to him.

"So are you going to give me your number or what?" I asked, glancing up at Jack.

He looked like he'd just entered a surprise party.

"You're bold," he said. "I like that. Give me a piece of paper and I'll give you my math." He scribbled the digits onto the back of a "Dear John" letter I had written to Ryan nights before.

"I'll call you," I promised.

"Do that," he said.

And I ran out to meet the yogis.

That Sunday, I bought a nice bottle of $6.99 Chianti, threw on Bjork's *Post* to get ye ole confidence up, and then left Jack a semi-shaky-aspiring-to-be-sexy message that went something like this:

BEEEEEP.

"Uh hey . . . Jack. This is the deejay you met the other night, DJ Sophie. I'm calling to see if you wanted to do something this weekend. So let me know, okay? My number's 212-555-904—"

BEEEEEP.

"Four."

BEEEEEP.

Oh, shitter. Did he get the last digit? I held the phone in my hand like a grenade. Was I in a cartoon or something? What luck! I wanted to fling the phone out the window. Instead, I took a deep breath. He got it, I assured myself and hell, even if he didn't I couldn't call back. Could I? I held the phone for a few moments, debated and then put it away. The number 4 had taken on a life of its own.

The slow bastard waited two days to call me back and left a voice mail asking if I'd like to go ride bikes in the park; the Buena Vista Social Club's "Candela" was playing faintly in the background of his message. I saved his fuzzy voice over the Latin conga drum just so I could hear it again before bed. He had an instant and indiscernible draw on me.

Our first date felt like eons later, but it was really only Sunday. We reunited in Union Square. There was a four-piece mariachi band playing on the red clay steps facing the crowded yard and middle-aged people attempting a sloppy but sweet salsa. For a few seconds from across the block, I watched Jack looking for me on the street corner. I liked seeing the anticipation on his face. What was he looking for? I mean, *exactly*. Like the Church sing in "Under the Milky Way." I wanted to be his girl, his chocolate sundae with whipped cream and a cherry on top, his favorite Bob Dylan jam.

Everything was just possibility from that unwritten point. I walked up to him and standing on my tippy-toes, kissed his cheek gently. He smelled like freshly sliced lemons.

His beautiful green eyes (the ones I'd mentioned before), were the color of bright moss. Man, I wanted to lie down and roll around in those eyes. I wished I could see out of them. I promised to maintain my Michigan calm though, and let him lead that night. Try not to scare him off.

We decided to have a few cocktails at a hipster café across the park. It was filled with posturing models and actor wannabes. We shared a booth and talked about the disappearance of Digable Planets (who the deejay was playing in blocks), the collective fall of the Native Tongues crew, and about meeting that stormy night across the pond.

"Your face went like this when I asked for your phone number," I said, sucking in my cheeks and bugging my eyes like a little Macaulay Culkin.

He laughed.

"You caught me off guard. But it was cute."

"So were you like 'Is she gonna call?' "

He shrugged.

"Fine, don't tell me. Tell me something else about you."

"All right, but first let's admit you're not a hip-hop deejay."

I laughed.

"True," I said.

"I'm gonna guess you either work for a music label or you're a writer."

"Not bad," I surmised. "You must have thought about it."

He nodded.

We stared at each other for a few moments. My heart felt like it was going to peel open.

"I'm a writer, you're correct."

He smiled.

"Okay," he laughed. "Now back to me."

I could hardly pay attention to his talk about wanting to be a graphic designer and growing up in a middle-class New Jersey American-Italian *famiglia.* I just mostly watched his lips forming the words. It was all too much to take in.

Although Jack came across as harmlessly juvenile (the kind of boy who still sticks potato chips in the middle of his ham sandwich), bursting with annoying bravado (that he didn't seem to buy either), he also seemed impressively kind, un-effeminately sensitive, and interestingly intricate. Full of potential, as we girls like to say. In a sea of disenchanted and jaded New Yorkers, he was a fresh pack of Doublemint gum.

I dug his laid-back Brooklyn boy thing, his slouchy athletic socks and black canvas Converse, Manhattan Portage bag, college study, and love of Frida Kahlo, and from the way he kept smiling after I finished a sentence, I sensed he liked things in me too. I privately declared him my first metropolitan treasure. We ordered some food.

"You should open up more, Sophie. You're really interesting."

I looked at his hands. Alive with veins and rushing blood. He was a charmer. *Stay on my arm,* The Smiths would implore.

"I am?" I asked, though I had a suspicion he was right.

"Yeah, you came to NYC by yourself. Set up shop. Have a good job, are independent . . . "

"Oh stop," I said, waving him on.

"You're hot and you're funny and smart."

"Thanks, thanks, and thanks. I'm flattered—seriously."

"Plus, you've got a fat booty and I like that." He wiggled his eyebrows and grinned like a Cheshire cat.

I kicked him.

"Ouch," he laughed, doubling over.

"You're really something," I smiled, crossing my arms.

He bent down to massage his shin.

"You should've played soccer 'cause you've got quite a kick there, girl."

"Well, one, my feet are huge. And two, actually I did play soccer in high school, but mostly I warmed the bench with my"—(I cleared my throat here)—"fat booty because the girls on the team were, like, so amazing."

He nodded, leaning over the table.

"In fact, one of them went on to be part of the Women's World Cup Championship team at twenty-three."

"No way," he said.

"Way. It's quite a humbling experience when you see one of your old classmates on the cover of *Time* magazine."

He nodded.

"See what I mean? You always got something interesting to say. I could listen to you talk forever. Tell your stories. Though some are fabricated. Like the deejay one."

I looked him over. How'd he know all the right things to say? Did he really like me as much as I did him? Or was he just gassing me up to get me in his bed? I was having so much fun being in his company, I hardly cared.

After a final White Russian, Jack asked me to share his side of the booth, so I did with pleasure. He asked me if I was dating any other guys and I said "not at this moment," which I meant literally and in general.

"What about you? Are you dating other girls?" I asked, feeling nervous.

He itemized a number of girls he was seeing.

". . . Persephone, Venus, and Sascha. Just five."

"Wow, you get around," I said, thinking of Jack's lucky ladies with their fancy art school names. His list seemed shitty but honest, so I just shrugged. I'd learned that, unfortunately, in New York City, dating multiple people at a time was common. This made navigating the tricky dating scene almost impossible.

"All you gotta do," he said sliding his arm over my shoulder, "is win me over from them." I rolled my eyes, but I liked the tease. It wasn't dangerous and consequential yet. He was simply living up to his slippery Sagittarius status.

"No problem, just stick with me kid," I said, spooning some of his garlic mashed potatoes into my mouth. I tried to match his breezy quality, so when I heard a dance hall song that I loved come on, I sidelined our conversation for a moment and just bounced my knee. My fingertips were starting to smell like Sicily.

After the song ended, all I wanted to do when I looked back at Jack was kiss him, so we left and I took his hand and led him to a bench in the park. He just filled me all the way up. There were a couple of bums hanging around, but they didn't bother us. We sat arm in arm and made out. I couldn't conceive a better New York moment. We were a Blondie song, on our way to a real Leonard Cohen coupling.

Jack and I linked again the following Saturday, and I was dying to see him. We made plans to hit yet another party in Brooklyn, this time in DUMBO, and I said I would meet him at the spot, but he insisted on picking me up in the city and taking me back himself so I "wouldn't get lost."

When we returned on the train together from Manhattan back to BK, we stopped by his loft apartment to drop off my stuff and make some phone calls to his friends. He pulled out an overpopulated janitor keychain to open the door.

"I don't know why I still keep all these keys," he said, turning the knob, the metal pieces rattling together.

"Maybe you like collecting things," I said, remembering Persephone, Venus, and Sascha.

Jack was in the bathroom when I noticed a couple of Polaroids laid out on a table of him and a plain-looking girl with pale skin and a strawberry blond pageboy cut. They were holding firecrackers and in one photo, their cheeks were touching. He had a big stupid grin on his face. The kind that screamed, "I'm having the goddamn time of my life!" I tucked the photos into a sketch notebook and walked to the fridge for some water, telling myself it didn't matter.

We danced at the party to the Pharcyde's "Passin' Me By" and snuck up to the roof a few times to make out—the twinkle of Manhattan in the distance. By the end of the night, I was nursing a Corona in the corner and watching Jack drunk-dancin' all by himself. There were a couple of women left on the floor doing their thing and he was smiling at me, snapping his fingers like Ol' Blue Eyes performing "Mack the Knife" and swinging his hips, his body bathed in a pale orange spotlight. His moves were charming and unself-conscious.

Tribe's "Everything Is Fair" came on, and Jack kept waving me over to join him, but I held back. I was picturing the photo of him and the girl, trying to figure out where she fit into the scene at hand. Maybe he was holding her tightly under his skin, layered in his heart? I strained to get X-ray vision. I was afraid of him and his secrets. Unsure I could be enough to satisfy him and keep up with him on the floor.

Jack approached me doing the Cabbage Patch.

"Are you having fun?" he asked, raising his eyebrows and switching to the Running Man.

"Watching you relive every dance move from the eighties? Yeah, I feel like I'm back at the roller rink."

He laughed, accidentally spilling some beer out of his plastic cup.

"Pouring some out for the homies," he slurred.

I shook my head.

"Well, Jack, I believe all you have left in your arsenal now is the Hokey-Pokey." I crossed my arms over my chest.

"Hey, you don't have to dare me to have a good time." He tapped my nose with his pointer finger.

"Clearly," I mouthed as he turned away. He was kind of clueless, but I liked it. I admired it almost. Oblivious, Jack shuffled, popped and locked himself right back into the middle of the floor. My affection was growing like a sea monkey.

Man, I liked him a lot from that distance and maybe it was the beer, but I decided right then that I wanted to sleep with him, even though I'd never done *that* before. He made me feel easy.

We went back to his place and I was a bit more boozed up than I thought and Jack said he didn't want to have sex with me, so we just passed out holding hands and listening to Portishead.

In the morning, he asked me if I wanted to grab some breakfast, but I said I should get home, even though I had nothing to do. So he gave me a spare toothbrush and we brushed our chompers together in the mirror, white foam collecting around our mouths. He walked me to the NR and we kissed bye through the bars. He said, "I love kissing you," and I heard the train coming so I ran away.

After that date, we spent one whole hot and humid week trading frustrated messages and a promise of a Saturday night on the town with our friends that, logistically, never panned out. But I knew we'd get together again soon. I was blissing and he was playing it cool, I told myself. Just be patient and he'll be back. How could he resist?

all jacked up

I'd been conducting some intense Internet research on Wyclef Jean and Haiti for a measly-paying *BeatMaker* freelance piece to be published in their "Personal Is Political" Election issue when my cell startled me. I thought it was Jean's publicist finally returning my press request.

"Hey Sophie, it's Jack."

I dropped my pen.

"Hey, Jack." I yearned to seem unfazed. "What up?"

"Just calling to say hey. What are you doing?"

"Right now?" I leaned back into my chair and stared at the entertainment website on screen. "Working."

"Boldly Beautiful?"

"No, no, no. That's a long story."

"Well, maybe you can tell it to me this weekend."

"This weekend?" I sat upright.

"We're celebrating my sister's thirtieth birthday at Sunday dinner."

"In Jersey?"

"Yeah."

"G'head."

"So, do you want to come?"

"Me?"

He laughed.

"Yeah, *you*. It'll be fun. My mom's cooking and everyone will be there."

I was suspicious, but went with it.

"Sure. Of course. Sounds lovely."

I pictured a table of meatballs, prosciutto, and Italian sausage, and me telling Jack's mom I'm an herbivore.

"I'll pick you up around four and we can take a cab to the PATH."

"Okay. I'll look forward to it," I said.

The weekend couldn't come fast enough. I spent some of my severance on a new BCBG black dress and red ballet flats. I dyed my roots and got a blow out. My nerves were on high.

Jack was on time and dressed in a blue button-up that complemented his olive skin. He was carrying a laundry bag like Santa Claus.

"You look beautiful," he said when I was locking up.

"Thanks. You clean up nice, too. But, just one thing I gotta get off my chest about tonight."

He nodded.

"For the sake of being self-protective, can we keep it on the friends tip?"

He shrugged.

"You're da boss."

That was news to me.

"And also—"

"That's two things, Sophie."

"Let's get your mom some flowers at the bodega."

An hour later, Jack and I were smushed around an oval table with his mom, dad, sister Dina, brother Anthony, and a couple teenage cousins visiting from The Boot. Candles were lit, and Andrea Bocelli was playing in the background. On the wall across the room, there were framed photos of the kids playing sports, performing in school plays, graduating.

I noticed a big one underneath the 3-D Virgin Mary statue. It looked like an elementary school photo of Jack, complete with a tropical background and about three teeth to his name. So cute and dorky.

"Sophie, are you Catholic?" the mother asked.

I set down my glass of wine and coughed.

"Uhhh," I stalled.

"Damn, Mom, why you putting my date on blast like that?"

"Blast?" Her face crinkled. "What kind of jive talk is that?"

"Don't embarrass the girl, Carla," the dad said.

"Or me! Jesus Christ," Jack huffed.

"Since when do you take the Lord's name in vain?" Mama asked loudly, her eyes bulging. Even I was scared.

Chaos broke out. I couldn't get a word in edgewise. Voices grew, overlapping one another, rising in volume. Frantic, I ejected from the table and proclaimed,

"I'm Greek Orthodox, and I'm a vegetarian!"

The Morettis ceased yapping. I sat back down. Jack started laughing and wiped my forehead with a napkin.

"That's my girl," he said.

"Feisty," Anthony surmised.

Mama Carla winked at me and, under the table, Jack cupped his hand over my bare knee.

"Dina, pass Sophie the broccoli and salad," the dad said.

Weirdly, it felt like I was right at home.

"So Jack told us you work at *Boldly Beautiful*. I subscribe," Dina said, her long airbrushed nails clawing the air.

"Really? That's cool," I said, feeling like a fugazi.

We endured some awkward silence. Dina went to fetch more vino. The visitors whispered in Italian. I ate broccoli.

"Jack's father made the dessert," Mama beamed.

"Don't worry, no meat," Papa said, laughing.

I smiled. I knew where Jack got his dry sense of humor.

"I'm sure it'll be wonderful. Everything is."

"Thank you, dear," Mama said.

"So, do you live in an overpriced warehouse like my trendy little bro?" Anthony asked. Jack punched him in the arm.

"And you all wonder why I haven't brought a girl to the house," he said, slicing his meatball like a surgeon.

"Did I say something wrong?" Anthony asked, provoking more heated opinions.

The table erupted again, this time louder with fists waving. One of the Italian cousins started choking on a lamb bone, so that got everyone's attention.

Jack rolled his eyes.

"Our children are all so special to us, but Jacky is my baby. My bambino," Carla said, pretending everything was normal again. Or maybe not pretending . . .

Jack smiled to her. Anthony grunted and Dina drank more wine.

"So spoiled," the sister said.

"Yeah, how'd you manage to score a lady like Sophie?"

"He hasn't told her about doing his laundry and cooking every night," Dina tossed in.

I turned to Jack.

"Well, I might not get another date after tonight." Jack clapped his hands around the table "Bravo. Brava."

We all shared a laugh and moved onto the tiramisu. Then, a three-layer birthday cake. We serenaded Dina, and Mama Carla begged for grandchildren. Dina reminded Mama of her recent painful breakup with some fella named Frank.

After dinner, Jack and I stood out on the Moretti front porch and took in the stars. He wrapped his arm around me.

"Does this violate the friends treaty?"

I shook my head.

"I don't care," I said.

"You know, my family really likes you. I can tell."

"They're precious."

"And insane, but yeah. I love 'em."

"I feel like I've seen a whole new side to you, Jacky."

"Ha, ha."

I leaned into him.

"I guess I am a big baby, but what can I say?"

"It must be hard to grow up."

He grinned.

"I'm glad you came out."

"I'm glad you asked."

He pecked my cheek.

"Just hope you don't disappear on me again."

I waited a galaxy for a reply.

"Me either." He said, arching his neck to the sky.

In that perfect, fleeting moment, even looking at the constellations together didn't seem cheesy.

I tried to sleep that night after Jack dropped me off, but I kept waking up to think of how much fun I'd had at the Morettis' house. And just how much hurt I'd set myself up for because of it.

be easy

I wanted Jack to come through. All the way. Be ready and sure of us—100 percent confident to proceed. I wanted him to call me up the next day and tell me he'd had so much fun with me and that he couldn't wait to see me again, but my phone never rang. Instead, I got a vague e-mail that read:

"Dear Sophie, hope you had fun at my sister's birthday. Don't listen to a word they said about me. My brother was just jealous that I brought home a beautiful girl. I miss you. Let's get together sometime soon."

I wrote him back:

"Thanks, Jack. Dinner was wonderful. What are you up to this weekend?"

No answer. Just that hollow, dark space that is the Internet. My message floating around in limbo; the phrase "sometime soon" pestering me like a fly.

That weekend I guilted Lucy into accompanying me to The Roots show at the Bowery Ballroom.

"I have an extra ticket and I wanted you to come," I told her over the phone.

"Why don't you take the new guy?" she asked.

"I'd love to, but he hasn't returned my e-mail or called."

"Okay, we'll go," thankfully avoiding the painful subject of me getting dissed. "You're turning me into a real hip-hop fan, you know."

"It's *y'know,*" I corrected. "Contract and slur, remember?"

"Got it, *chica*. Contract and slur," she giggled.

At the show, Lucy and I sauntered to our balcony seats, double-fisting five-dollar Bud Lights in plastic cups and rating hot b-boys on the way. The instant we sat down, I spotted Jack from the balcony. Like magic. Destiny. He was on the mezzanine, smack-dab in the middle of the floor. Instinct took over and I immediately called down to him. He turned around from his group of friends, looked up, mouthed my name, and waved.

"That's the guy?" Lucy said, sounding awestruck.

"Yeah," I cooed.

"That guy?" she asked, pointing.

I lowered her arm.

"He looks different from that night at the party," she said.

"He's a cutie. Sweet too," I said, accidently inhaling a cloud of white froth from my Bud into my nose.

"Then why isn't he up here with you?"

"I don't know . . . because . . . he runs away." I wiped my nose with a napkin. "But he'll come around." I stirred my beer with my finger to calm it down.

"As long as you're happy, Sophie," she shrugged.

Happy? Please. Love was agony, torture—a battlefield, in the perennial words of Pat Benatar. My hands were clamming up. I licked my finger.

"Look Lucy, you go for the older, more established, seasoned man. I'm more into the man-boy type."

"Clearly," she laughed. "He's wearing a backpack."

"Snob," I said, pinching her thigh.

She nudged me.

"He looked glad to see you," she said with sincerity.

The house lights dimmed and I chugged my watery beer. This afflicted me with the hiccups for the whole show. I watched the back of Jack's head bobbing in the crowd. It was a beautiful bobbing head. Hiccup.

When I got home after the show, he'd left me a message on my answering machine.

"Hey, Sophie, it's Jack. I missed you after seeing you tonight. Let's get a drink tomorrow. Call me, please."

He said *please,* I repeated joyously. I felt victorious and instantly picked up the phone.

The next night we got together at an East Village dive. We shared a lumpy couch and told crappy jokes and talked about our summer regrets. He said he was really happy to see me, and I believed him because I could see it in his fat smile. I said I felt the same way, but it seemed sort of ridiculous that we had to wait. I didn't want to think our recent separation was because of a good reason, like say, another woman or women to whom Jack was attached. As my brother had recalled on the phone the day before,

"Denial ain't a river in Egypt." Harsh, but I probably needed some tough love.

Jack slipped his fingers through mine and smelled the back of my hand. Then he told me that, next month, he was going to San Diego to visit the girl from the photo (he actually *spoke* her name, which I can't repeat out loud, but it rhymed with "cockroach." Just kidding. It was Jenny.)

Sunny muthafuckin' Jenny. A California girl with, I was certain, big plump happy tits that could squash my sad, city-girl 34Bs. I felt a cold fist tightening around my neck. In a rare occurrence, I didn't have anything to say, so I pretended like I didn't hear anything and didn't even care. I'm no fool, I told myself. I'm totally smarter than this guy.

The word-fast lasted all of about eight seconds.

"Me and Jenny kind of go back, but only officially started dating about a month before I met you. Before she left."

"Did I ask?" I snapped.

"No," he replied. "But I do want to be honest with you."

If he was trying to be nice to me, then why was I fighting an instinct to sock him?

"Fine. Thanks for the information." I twirled the ends of my hair and slurped my vodka-cranberry through a thin straw.

"She's a big part of my history, okay?" He was defensive.

"Great. Good for you guys." I slapped his knee.

"Don't be mad."

"I'm not. It's just frustrating that you're telling me this now. I don't know how it changes us or how you want me to react."

"We're seeing other people while we're long distance. She's just in the picture, that's all." He sighed, looking me dead in the eyes.

"Literally," I responded.

He skimmed the edge of my jean skirt with his fingertips and tickled my knee.

"Don't," I chided, pushing his hand away.

"I do care about you, Sophie. I think about you all the time," he said.

I bit my lip and gave him a thorough once over.

"I know, Jack. I believe you." My anger was dissipating. Defeated, I leaned in and kissed his lips as if the physical contact would solve something.

That sticky 80-degree night, we went to my place, turned my fan on high, lit candles in the corners of my room, and put Miles on repeat. The music helped me to relax, let go, give in to the moment and not worry about later, about living as forgettable #2. Jack started kissing up my thighs and sweat beads gathered on the backs of my knees. I thought of him taking off on that plane and what's-her-name meeting him gleefully at the gate. It made my tummy hurt.

As 4 a.m. neared, we lay in my bed making animal shadows on the wall, the sounds of the street finally becoming quiet. Then Jack said he had to go, but didn't move. "The problem is," he said, making a bird, "I don't want to leave."

I nodded.

"It just might be awhile before I see you again, Sophie."

Breathe. I got up and put on my Madonna Blonde Ambition Tour T-shirt, not saying anything. Then a few minutes later, he was gone. Again.

But for the next week, Jack and I ran into each other all over the island—at the subway stop on Broadway, on Third Avenue by the bookshop, by his art school and each time this would happen, we'd shake our heads feigning disbelief, chat and then walk away. If a greater force was trying to tell us something, then after the fourth time of crossing paths, we got the message and made a definite plan to get together on the approaching Saturday night, two weeks before his San Diego departure.

When I hung up the phone with Jack, I got the sense that, as turtle daters, we were about to hit either water or the highway. As a tragic Leonard Cohen song, we were checking out of the Chelsea Hotel.

I stayed in my apartment all day watching a preseason football game, painting my toenails blood red, chain-smoking Marlboro Lights and then taking a long, steamy shower. We had plans to grab a few drinks and when he rang my buzzer promptly at 8:30 p.m. to pick me up, I skipped to the door.

I planted one on his cheek and he said I looked pretty. We opened the bottle of Merlot he brought and sat next to each other on my couch, our knees touching intently. As we were about to leave my apartment, he kissed me in the kitchen, stove dials pressing into the small of my back. Then we walked hand in hand on the downtown streets, swinging our arms together.

At the bar, I asked him if he loved the cross-country chick and he said he thought he did, but he wasn't sure. I told him that I couldn't keep seeing him since he had feelings for her and he nodded solemnly. I said it had just become a little too hard for me, and he said it was hard for him, too. I jutted my chin and told him that

I needed a boy who was all about me, and he said he'd wanted to be that boy, but he and the Cali girl had made a serious turn before she went West and that he's only twenty-three and he's confused. Me goddamn too, I thought.

"Jenny was my first love when we were in high school. She dated my boy back then so we couldn't be . . . " he drifted off. "Let's just say we've been through a lot."

"Look, I'm sure you're supplying these gory details in an effort to be real with me, but it's not helping. I don't want to hear anymore."

"Who knows what will happen? Maybe you and I will end up together." He stared off into blankness, so content to just let his destiny unfold. I wanted to bang him in the head with a pot.

"Open-ended statements like that can really hurt if you don't mean them, Jack."

"But, I do," he said. "I do," he whispered. "I don't know how to explain it."

"Well, nothing's going to change on these terms."

I wanted to bawl, crawl under the bar, and hide, but I knew someone had to make a firm choice and that as much as I liked to ignore reality, when it was shot dead and lying limp right in my lap, it was impossible to do so. Even for a John Lennon dreamer like me.

Jack told me that night we met back at the party, he'd stared at me from the minute I walked in and it took all the nerve he could muster to come up and flip records next to me. He said that after I took his number, he spent two days wondering if I'd call him and then when I did, he listened to my message five times. My eyes were starting to get blurry so I nudged him and asked, "Only five?"

We went back to my apartment that night, messed around a bit and fell asleep. I didn't know what was happening, so I just let it all go. In the morning I took his picture with my beat-up Pentax 35mm, propped on my pillow, while he told me that he was glad that we'd had that talk the night before.

On the way out the door, he asked me if he should "forget" his wallet in my bedroom so he could have an excuse to see me again, and I said, no he couldn't and that you weren't supposed to tell the person when you did it anyway.

Then we walked to get breakfast and he asked me if I thought we'd bump into each other anymore and I said I didn't think so.

In the booth, over runny eggs and busted-open jelly packets, we talked about the abysmal future and our respectively rowdy Mediterranean families and high art and book covers and what we were going to do that Sunday. There was a pit in my belly, but I picked at my food.

I took his hand across the table and noticed his cuticles were gnawed. I told him that it looked like that hurt and he said, "I get nervous," and snatched his hand back. To lighten the mood, I jokingly serenaded him with the chorus to "I Used to Love Him," subbing in "like" for the more intense version of feeling. He smiled weakly and said in a whisper,

"Well, I guess it's good we didn't make it to 'love,' right?"

I shrugged.

Please do not go was the only thing on my mind that morning. The only four true words my lips longed to form. Just like that Violent Femmes song. What if I never saw him again?

We left the diner and kissed a casual good-bye on the street corner.

"I'll call you," he said. "We'll keep in touch."

Famous last words, I thought.

Sometimes we don't love the right guy for us; for confirmation of this, I listened to Bonnie Raitt and Sheryl Crow and cried every night for one week straight. It was also the first time I'd lost my appetite over a boy; unfortunately, I couldn't find any songs addressing this disturbing issue.

Then one night on the phone, Lucy hypothesized another scenario:

"Forget him, Sophie. He's dating all these girls and it sounds like he might even have a serious girlfriend now. He's a player. Plain and simple."

Which meant I had been played. This theory almost made me want to commit that Japanese form of ritual suicide where you cut out your own stomach.

"But he didn't even get to third base with me," I countered.

"Doesn't matter, it's just about the game."

I sighed.

"I wasn't good enough, that's all." I told Lucy, wiping my nose with my sweatshirt sleeve. "Somebody should just say it."

I was a speed bump in his life. And, ultimately, a reconfirmation of his devotion to another girl. Naturally, Lucy disagreed and blamed the entire, seed-spreading male species (a sweeping judgment that didn't resonate for me since I hadn't reached the angry stage of abandonment yet) and got mad at me for even thinking that it was my fault.

"Screw him," she said with steadfast loyalty, "he wasn't even that hot." But we both knew at that unforgiving point, Jack could have looked like a mushroom and I would have still wanted him.

That next Monday in my photo class, I made a contact sheet of my film and saw Jack's face in a tiny box in the top row. An unexpected thing happened when I looked at him captured by my lens, I felt the subtlest sprinkle of resentment at him for deserting me. Lucy had been right: Fuck him. Life goes on. More fish in the sea. And other useful aphorisms came to me.

I put the dripping sheet in the fixer tray and then walked outside into the bright light where my salt and pepper–haired professor was sitting in a school desk.

"Nice shot," he said. I half-smiled, shifting my feet. "It's just a little light." He gave me the tray back.

"Two more seconds," he said tapping his cane as I turned to walk away, "and you got him."

I paused at the entranceway and hung my head. Then I walked down that dark hall and tossed the photo back into the iridescent water.

I loved that gentle, muted picture of Jack that spoke for all the things we couldn't be, but after the first long week apart, I decided to tuck it away in a corner of my closet next to a beat-up pair of green Pumas and move on.

I should have known it was probably doomed: after our first date, Jack had snail-mailed me a homemade mixtape filled with "You Got Me" by The Roots, Isaac Hayes's "Walk On By," and "You Look Like Rain" by Morphine. Yet many of those beautiful and emotive songs had been amputated at their ends because Jack, I deduced, just couldn't wait to get to the next one.

what's beef?

I decided the way to push through my love dilemma was by throwing myself back into work. I did a spec story for *Beat-Maker,* covering Talib Kweli's first live solo show at SOB's, where mixmaster prodigy DJ Hi-Tek told me his beats sounded like "cherry Kool-Aid." I then spent a whole afternoon trying to translate that mumbo-jumbo quote into the perfect intro 'graph.

Reluctantly, I also had to attend my last day at *Boldly Beautiful.* My dramatic "shock and awe" departure left cubicle neighbors and coworkers mystified. As I nonchalantly packed my boxes, I slyly avoided questions about why I was leaving "so suddenly" by channeling the Bill Clinton strategy: "It depends on what your definition of 'leaving' is." This left even nosy reporters too dumbfounded to pry further.

Sam haphazardly organized a champagne and chocolate dipped strawberries farewell in the conference room and Claire, ridden with remorse, sent me off with a killer reference letter. HR matched my firing with one-month severance.

I also starting hanging out with Furious: hitting up Thursday's hip-hop night at the Latin Quarter, buying vinyl at Fat Beats, sharing shrimp fried rice at Noodles & Zen Sum in Chinatown. I got to submerge myself into the hip-hop scene with a partner.

One personality trait I did admire about Furious was that for all his "I-just-don't-give-a-fuck" b-boy baloney, he was also the most polite person I'd ever met. At a restaurant, he'd hold the door open for little old ladies, he'd always walk me to the train, pay for my cover or drinks, end or start his sentences with a soft "thank you" or tender "please." He was holding the chivalry movement together. Plus, I could tell he really liked me.

"I wanna show you something, Sophie."

I eyed him from across the table. It was pizza night at Ray's in the Lower East Side.

"Like what?" I asked, fearful.

He unzipped his messenger bag and pulled out a copy of *Beat-Maker* with Gang Starr on the cover and the title "The Kings of the Underground" splashed across it.

He slid the magazine across the table.

"I don't think I've seen this issue yet," I said, holding it before me.

"Yeah, be careful, it's fresh."

" 'Who Will Take Over the Throne?' " I read from one of the headlines.

"Flip to page sixty-five."

I fanned the pages in front of me.

"Is my Wyclef story in here? I thought it was coming out in the next issue," I said.

"I didn't see it, nah. Did you get to page sixty-five yet?"

"Hold up," I stopped on the page. "On The Come Up," I read aloud. The photo spread featured rappers and deejays sitting on wooden blocks and plastic crates in what looked to be a damp, dark basement—lots of blues and grays and concrete. Smack dab in the middle of the page—sandwiched in between DJ Hi-Tek and a white emcee named Eyedea—was none other than Furious.

And when I say sandwiched, I mean it.

"Awwww," I said, looking across the table where he was waiting for my reaction. "You're on the crease." His face and body were chopped in half by the magazine's binding. I slid my finger up and down the spine.

"I know, it's dope, isn't it?"

But you're on the crease.

"I mean, it sucks that I'm in the middle, but shit, I'm there. And I'm already getting calls about it. From major labels."

"Really? That's great," I said. And it was.

"It's all coming in line," he said, rubbing his hands together.

There was a sparkle in his eye and it was pretty exciting to be sharing some of his shine.

"Tonight there's an open mic down the street at Baby Jupiter's, and a Sureshot Records exec is coming to see me perform." He patted his chest. "Me."

"I wanna come," I said.

"Cool," he answered, taking the magazine back.

He had what we call Heat. It was fun to feel his warmth. Mooch some of his glory. Bask in it.

"So, I got a question now," he said.

I sank down in my booth, leaning back.

"I think I ate too much pizza," I said, grumbling and rubbing my stomach.

"Can I ask you a question? I'm dead-ass serious now."

"Yes, sir," I saluted.

"You dating someone?"

"Are you asking if I got a man?"

He laughed.

"Yeah, that's it." He unwrapped a toothpick and twirled it in his mouth.

I thought about Jack.

"No. I was seeing somebody, but it didn't work out."

"Why?"

"Why? Well, maybe you can provide some insight on that one. Some male perspective."

I told him the story of finding the photo on the desk and the Cali girl and how Lucy thought he was a player.

"Nah," Furious shook his head. "He sounds like he doesn't know what he wants, but he ain't a player."

"No?" I asked.

He shook his head again.

"A real player woulda put those photos away, Sophie."

I smiled.

"You know what, you're probably right."

He nodded.

"Trust me. I am."

"How would you know that sneaky stuff anyway?" I asked.

"Back in the day, I was kinda like that."

" 'Back in the day,' huh? Like last week?"

"No, I'm reformed." He said, smoothing down his Phat Farm T-shirt.

I was skeptical. Rappers, singers, musicians were legendary for their womanizing. Just look at Mick.

"I concentrate on my music now. I'm gonna blow up and be a big star and I'm gonna buy my mom a house somewhere nice, like maybe Jersey City or East Orange. In-Sha-Allah." He clapped his hands together and looked up to heaven.

"It'll happen, Furious. And then all the hoochies will come running."

"I'm not sweating it."

"So now do I get to ask you a question?"

"Aight."

"What the hell is your real name? Tell me, please."

He shook his head and looked down at his watch.

"Furious is so 'grrrrrr.' "

"We gotta go, babe. I'll square up the check and let's bounce."

"Fine," I said, rising from the table. "But don't forget I am a journalist and I will find out."

He put his arm around me as we went to pay.

"Ohh, I'm so scurred," he laughed and faked a shiver.

"Shut up," I said, pushing him away.

Since Furious was an "up-and-coming star," according to *Beat-Maker,* we got VIP treatment at the clubs, he laced me with a new cell phone, and I even went with him to the record label offices when he signed his deal.

But then one night, at Furious's apartment, the weather changed. While I was waiting for him to finish up in the shower, I found a piece of scrap paper on his desk under his fuzzy Kangol cap. In graffiti-like letters it read: "RHYME FOR A DIME: How do you put down/What words can't explain/A girl with a smile that'll getcha high as a plane/She smells like sugar but tastes like rain."

"'High as a plane'?" That was Writing Rhymes 101. I called Lucy quietly to dish.

"Dooohoood," I said giggling.

I read her the lyrics. She said it was "retarded." I fought for "corny." We settled on "pathetic." I played with a Trick Daddy ashtray on his desk.

"Yup, I can really pick them," I sighed. Then, in a Darren-Star-dramedy-turn-of-events, I looked up from the receiver only to find Furious standing and dripping in a towel by the entranceway to his room. He didn't even look angry, just completely crestfallen.

"I gotta go, Lucy." I hung up on her and gulped.

I felt like an ass and tried immediately apologizing but he just said I should leave. Then he added an emphatic "please."

"We were just being stupid. We were totally kidding."

"Yeah, I know." He hadn't moved deeper into the room.

I thought about how much I knew rap meant to him. How serious he was about it. The rhyme wasn't even that bad in hindsight.

"I wrote it about you—because I liked you. Damn." He rubbed his head and wiggled his toes like a little kid.

I recognized the past tense.

"Me? I'm so sorry, Furious. I feel really bad about hurting your feelings."

"Just leave pl—"

I held up my hand.

"Don't say it. I don't deserve the polite pleasantries." I zipped up my bubble-goose. "I'm out."

He ignored my e-mails and phone calls for a few days, and I really started to miss him. We'd had a lot of fun together: He took me out and introduced me to important people in the business, and the truth was, after all that, he hadn't even tried to put a move on me. I'd blown it.

Finally, my phone rang.

"May I speak to Sophie Drakas please?"

"This is she," I answered, returning the formal.

"Hey, it's Charlotte from *BeatMaker*. Dana wanted to talk to you. Can you hold the line?"

"Sure," I said. Those few silent seconds felt like forever.

"Sophie," Dana said.

My body jolted.

"Hey, Dana, how are you?"

"I'm cool. Listen, let's cut to the chase."

"Okay," I said and started nibbling on my fingernails.

"We loved your Wyclef Jean piece. The copy was clean, you made your deadline, and you proved your heart is in your writing. We think you'd make an amazing addition to our *BeatMaker* team. What do you say?"

I was in shock. It felt like a piano had dropped onto my head.

"Sophie?"

"Yeah," I said, regaining my balance. "Definitely. Thank you."

"Can you come in this afternoon? We'll set you up with HR and show you around the offices."

I looked at the clock on the stove. 12:13 p.m.

"I'll be there," I said.

"See you," she said. "I gotta get back to the grind."

"Thanks again." I hung up the phone and started jumping up and down in the air, yelping at the top of my lungs until I was out of breath (about six seconds) and went to have a peaceful smoke by the window to really savor the moment.

I love this city! I'm in New York and I'm making it! I wish I could give Manhattan a big kiss! I looked at my window frame and thought about putting my lips to the dusty building but it was too weird. All I could think was, this is the best, most exciting city in the world. And I get to live in it. I get to LIVE in it.

I stubbed out my cigarette, which had taken me about thirty seconds to smoke, and raced to my bedroom.

When I arrived at the *BeatMaker* offices, I took in the difference between it and *Boldly Beautiful*. Firstly, the receptionist was about forty years younger, with clear, caramel skin and a raspy voice. The lobby was much smaller and all the strewn-about magazines on the table were past issues of *BeatMaker* with pictures of rappers, not models, on the covers. The coffee in the corner, on a folding card table, was self-serve and sort of overflowing with grinds.

When Dana came out to meet me, she was dressed in jeans, pointy heels, and a form-fitting cord blazer. Her features were almost Native American or Mexican—dark almond eyes, a round face with strong, high cheekbones and thick black hair. She wore tiny gold bamboo earrings that reminded me of ones I had in middle school. I followed her to the Editorial Section.

"We're gonna meet the editors you'll be working with. Of course, you already know a couple of them from your freelance pieces, but now you'll get to meet them face to face. More guys here than at *Boldly Beautiful,* I would imagine," she winked.

I nodded enthusiastically.

BeatMaker looked very similar to the Def Jam offices—messy, urban chic. Cubicle dividers in between the staffers and work spaces decorated with magazine clippings of bands and a surplus of CD piles. My new, bare desk was next to the window, in a cramped, cobwebbed corner next to the interns and this fact-checker named Rosalinda. She was playing Santana on her computer.

"Hi," I said, shaking Rosalinda's hand.

"Hola," she said, giving me her sweaty, limp palm. "Welcome to the neighborhood," she said.

"Thanks," I smiled.

I trailed Dana around the office, and she pointed out the fax machine, bathrooms, photo department.

"You remember Amon," she said, leaning into his glass office.

Amon looked up from the photo illuminator, holding a microscope.

"Hey, girl," he said, coming over and giving me a hug.

I gave him a good squeeze.

"What's shakin'?" I asked.

"Not much, just working," he answered. "By the way, I loved my J-division MP3," he said.

"Well, there's more where that came from."

"Sweet," he said. "Congratulations on the job."

"Thanks, you can take some credit for that."

"My pleasure," he said. "Stop in and see me again."

I nodded and Dana took me for more meet-and-greets.

Next she introduced me to HP, another associate editor with a big poster of Lauryn Hill duct-taped above his desk.

"I love Lauryn Hill," I said, after shaking his hand.

HP smiled.

"I don't know how people can like that Jafaican," a guy yelled from the other side of the office. All three of us turned in his direction.

"What did he say?" I asked in a hushed voice.

"Ignore him, that's Smith. One of our photo researchers," HP laughed. "Yo, stop doggin' my girl!" HP threw a wad of paper over the cubicle, and Smith, tall, thick, and looking like a big, overstuffed football player/teddy bear, stood up.

"Lauryn's from Jersey not Jamaica. Okay, face it."

We all laughed.

"And this is Smith," Dana said, leading me his way.

"Sophie's our new associate editor."

"Hey," I said.

"Hey," he replied, suddenly serious. Then he went back to his work on the computer.

We moved onto Fred, the senior editor, a redhead with a gold-capped tooth and a love of drum-and-bass. Jenna, the production coordinator, who wore cornrows, faintly smelled of cinnamon and spoke softly. And Ethan, a photographer, who had that nerdy chic thing going on—thick black framed glasses, ironic gas station attendant shirt and red Sauconys. We ended up back at Dana's office.

"So, you can see we don't have a proper editor in chief at the moment," she said from behind her desk in her corner office.

"I noticed that," I answered, unscrewing the bottle of water she'd offered me.

"We're interviewing candidates at the moment, so I'm taking over the duties in the meantime. Acting E-I-C, if you will. We've got a small staff, but it's a talented group and they're hard workers."

I nodded.

"So, you know where your desk is. You've met the fam. I'm gonna pass you down to our HR person and if you have some time after that, come on up and set up your computer and voicemail. Okay?"

"Yes," I said, standing up. "Thanks again for everything, Dana."

"Sure, it's great to have you as part of the team, Sophie."

I knew *BeatMaker* was the place to shed my bench-warmer past and become a starter, a leader, a scorer.

you know my steez

My first official day as a full-timer at *BeatMaker,* an infamous ex-con and Latin rap record exec named Big Vega got livid about a story I'd written. I couldn't really blame him because the story was all just based on a rumor—that he'd just been incriminated by the Georgia authorities in the recent murder investigation of Chief, a nineteen-year-old Savannah rapper, gunned down outside a studio.

The problem was, I'd been directed to report on it by Fred and since I'd only been a staffer for a few hours, I couldn't very well say no. So I just posted the gossip as "Breaking News" on the magazine's Web site, hoping that it'd come true and breaking every journalistic ethics rule I'd ever been taught. *That's all.*

Within minutes of its launch, the advertising department called down to editorial requesting we remove the piece or, at the very least, rephrase it, before the label pulled all of their pages with our company. All I kept thinking was *shit.* Vega had built a Mafia-like empire on ruthless intimidation and criminal dealings.

I'd heard those exceptional but true tales of music journalists getting beaten up or banged over the head with a bottle of champagne for stories artists weren't exactly happy with and let me tell you, I wanted none of that. I mean, I used to work for *Boldly Beautiful* for God's sake . . . our biggest controversies had been over bangs. I had pragmatic limits and within hours as a hip-hop journalist, I'd crashed right into my first one.

While everyone else went to lunch at McDonald's, I made a chump move and secretly changed the byline on the story to "anonymous." Then I changed it back to my name again. Then, back to anonymous. My upper lip perspired and my digits felt numb, but it was the only way to get my own back. I wanted to live!

A few days later, I was assigned to a press day at the legendary Landmark Studios, buried in a grimy section of downtown Manhattan. The hit factory had a rep that loomed large in the industry; it was the O.G., owned by a cool white guy from Sunset Park who took zero bullshit. Almost every big dog in the game recorded a joint (and often a classic cut) within the magical soundproof walls of that place, so anyone who rode through agreed to follow the rules, if only that the good rap karma might bless them.

It was also just a chill-out spot for artists to holler at their friends and check out who was laying down the hot shit. Jenna, the production coordinator with cornrows, told me before I left the *BeatMaker* office that Landmark was so ghetto the vending machine in the lobby there "sells chips, soda, and Phillies Blunts."

She also kindly confided in me another Landmark story: she, a freelance photographer, and her assistant had recently gone over to shoot a producer for a big December Feature Well story. In the lobby, they'd clearly stated their name and affiliation to the receptionist who was "some young, regular white guy."

The kid quickly gave *BeatMaker*'s team access to set up their equipment, but after they'd started settling into the den area, a thuggish femcee spotted them and started flipping out on the receptionist for letting them in. She'd screamed that security in the studio was shit and that her crew might be in danger of attack while recording since access was so permissive.

"She was crazy. Cocking her fingers like a gun in his face screaming, 'Don't you know there are n-ggas out there who want to kill my boys?! Don't you?!'" Jenna paused. "Yo, it was deep," she finished, biting her lip.

I'd chewed off half a thumbnail at this point.

She said the poor boy had looked like he was going to cry. Jenna, a devout Southern Baptist, also said "effing" instead of "fucking." Then she totally bailed out on accompanying me to the press day. "Sorry," she said shaking her head. "I am *so* not going back there." *Super,* I thought, *send me solo.*

It was my second face-to-face interview, but this rapper, Hooky, was no Ja Rule. He was an underground emcee with a low profile and a determined group of obsessed fans who'd hunt down his music at mom-and-pop record shops. No wide distribution, no Hot 97 heavy rotation, no BET. Though he was less flashy, I was still nervous because Hooky presented a different challenge: I really had to know all the right details or his die-hard fans would ream me.

As though the interview, Jenna's cautionary tale, and Landmark's standing weren't enough to make a girl anxious, this was also where Noah (remember Jack's friend from those parties?)

worked part-time as a recording assistant. I was nervous, but a part of me was secretly wishing I'd run into him because he was a familiar face and he'd seemed pretty nice those couple of times we'd met.

Plus, early that morning, I'd woken up with a desperate, shameful need to hear Jack's voice, so I called his apartment, figuring he'd already be at work and his answering machine would pick up. (His taped voice would be still enough to satisfy me.) So while I was shuffling around in my PJs and dumping coffee grinds into the dripper, I dialed his number and heard a girl's voice on the machine. Thinking I had the wrong number, I hung up and dialed again and this time actually forced myself to listen to the high-pitched, cheery voice on the other end, saying, "You've reached Jack and Jenny. Leave us a message and we'll call you back."

I wanted to vomit. Between the name Jenny and the words "us" and "we" that emphasized their solidarity and union, I thought I would heave right there over the sink. It blew. Was he living with her now? I hung up before the question fell out of my mouth and onto their tape. But not before they probably heard a deranged person panting on the other end.

On that fateful Thursday morning, I'd picked out a Liz Claiborne red denim skirt to sport along with a fitted black cotton V-neck and black calf-high boots. My hair was blown straight and parted down the middle. My door knockers were from the eighth grade and lately, I kicked those every day. It was an attempt to look pretty without being too "frilly googoo gaga," in Lucy-speak. A decidedly thin line and as I walked into Landmark's building, I didn't know what side I ended up on.

The elevator was rickety, and I was running late for my interview. When the doors parted I was led into a hallway that was set in black light. The ambiance reminded me of stoner dorm rooms in college. There was graffiti on the right wall; the Landmark logo (a menacing dragon holding a stick of dynamite) was positioned smack dab in the middle of the mural. On top of the décor, it smelled like dirty socks and Nag Champa incense. Gang Starr's "You Know My Steez" was coming out of a scratchy speaker.

Directly in front of me was a tiny, rectangular bulletproof window with soft yellowish light shining through, the color of stained tea. I walked toward the frame and knocked lightly. A guy in a Patriots cap leaned forward and slid the glass to one side. His brown eyes were bloodshot.

"Yo."

That was a question.

"I'm Sophie. Here to meet . . ." I looked down at my notes. "Kevin."

He nodded and closed the window, then picked up the phone. I noticed pale orange freckles on the tip of his nose and on the apples of his cheeks. He cradled the phone in between his ear and shoulder. I could see his mouth making out my name.

He opened the glass.

"Sorry," he said in a husky voice. "Where are you from?" He coughed.

"Oh, *BeatMaker*."

He slid the glass again. And again.

"He'll be right out," he smiled coyly up to me as though it were the punch line to a joke. "I'm gonna buzz you in through that door." He pointed to my left.

"Okay, thank you," I said flashing a quick smile. I grabbed the doorknob wondering how many other cuties they hid behind these walls. Maybe it was the secret treasure chest us single gals had been searching for. This heady, attractive possibility kept my body moving forward.

I ran smack into Kevin, the owner, in the dark hallway.

"Hey, Sophie," he shook my hand firmly, looked down at the floor. "Can you wait in the family room until we call you? Hooky's in with *VIBE* now."

"Sure," I said, meeting Kevin's gaze again. I did as I was told and sat in front of the TV, against the back wall. There were couches on either side and rap videos on the set: a new Mystikal video for "Shake Ya Ass." There was a black kid in a do-rag draped over one couch. He looked about my age. I smiled to him and he hit me back with a brisk half-smile as though it were a favor.

Friendly.

"Hey," he said yawning.

I sat with my legs crossed as the freckle-faced boy entered the room. It'd been sometime since a new face had set my heart aflutter. He plopped down near me, moved an ashtray in between us and lit a Marlboro Light.

I had just quit and was trying to gauge whether boys found the nonsmoking me more attractive, as my brother had promised. But both guys just stared at the TV. A flashy video came on for an R&B song about a guy who pines for the woman who left him for his best friend.

"I'd fuckin' kill a girl for shit like that," the black boy said in my direction.

"Yeah, especially a wifey," the other added.

Outnumbered, I nodded.

The hot boy sat quietly chain-smoking and let the black kid do all the talking. He held each cigarette in between his thumb and index finger when he inhaled. After he exhaled he'd wave the smoke away from my direction. Each time he'd fan the air away, in my head I'd hear myself saying "thanks" and thinking scandalous thoughts simultaneously.

Nas's "The World Is Yours" video came on. I tapped my foot to the melodic chorus.

It didn't seem like they got many girls inside Landmark. You could almost smell the testosterone in the air, plus there were empty beer bottles all over, a pool table in the next room, and rap albums lining the walls. It was cold inside.

"Uh, where's the rest room?" I asked.

Freckle boy pointed down the long, dark hallway.

I nodded and lifted myself up. As I passed in between the guys, I stood up straight and sucked in my waist. Down the hall, I tried not to trip as the words *they're checking out my ass* repeated in my head.

I decided that when I got back to the room I'd ring Noah and ask him if he was working behind one of those doors.

When I returned to the family room, a couple other kids—one guy, one woman—had joined us. In their J. Crew fleece and Eddie Bauer shoes, they looked even more out of place than I. They'd just brought Chinese takeout and were taking out the cartons one by one from the paper bag.

"Remember, Hooky don't eat pork," freckle boy said.

They nodded.

"We'll give him the sautéed vegetables," the woman said. She had a Xerox copy of the press list on her lap and I noticed she'd dripped some red curry sauce on it. I reasoned that they were Hooky's publicists 'cause publicists always seem to be the ones responsible for artists getting their meals.

I moved to hallway, took out my cell, scrolled to Noah's name and my whole body turned into one giant sweat ball. I didn't know why I was so nervous.

"Hey, Noah, it's Sophie. Remember me?"

"Yeah, hey Sophie. What's up?"

"Oh, I'm just at Landmark for this Press Day and so, I just thought I'd call and see if you were here, too."

"Right, right. They're having it for Hooky, I remember. Actually, babe, it's my day off."

"Nice," I said meaning completely the opposite. "I just thought if you were around, but," I shook my head, "it's cool."

"Well, how long do you think you'll be there?"

"Um, hmm. Maybe like an hour or so."

"I can come up for a second and see you. I had to stop by the studio today anyway."

"I'd like that," I said smiling.

When I walked back, I got called into a recording studio to interview Hooky. My knees were knocking I was so nervous.

For all intents and purposes, this was my first *BeatMaker* rap interview as an official staffer. Suddenly, I couldn't remember if Wu-Tang was from New Jersey or Long Island, if Premier produced

Ready to Die or *Life After Death,* if Hooky had been on OutKast's *Southernplayalisticadillacmuzik* or Goodie Mob's *World Party.* Any facts that I had known went south and all my ignorance came to forefront.

What the hell was I doing here? Hooky would instantly smell the fakery on my clothes and devour me for munchies. I should've just stuck to writing copy about self-tanning creams and midseason TV replacements. I wanted to run back to the Vont$ cafeteria!

But I didn't. This here was the start of something I'd wanted my whole life so I walked faithfully forward and ignored my insecurities and the brain freezes.

When I got to the room, there was a skinny, dark-skinned Rasta-looking guy in a Bob Marley T-shirt sitting down behind the boards, staring off into space.

I knocked on the open door and he turned to me and smiled.

"Hey," I said, recognizing his face from my press pack. I moved to shake his hand. He smiled and said hey back.

We sat down together on a couch in front of an empty recording booth. I imagined what greats—Biggie, Pac, or Kane perhaps—had spit eternal, seminal rhymes into that giant microphone.

The room was eerily quiet. I opened my notebook.

"I actually did prepare questions to ask you."

"Aight," he said flatly.

I swallowed. I didn't want Hooky to think I was a novice know-nothing. I would own this interview, I silently cheered. Except then I dropped my microcassette recorder. He bent down and retrieved it for me.

"Thanks," I said, straightening out my skirt. "So, let's start." I turned my tape on. Suddenly, my recorded voice came blaring out!

"Testing one, two, three . . . Testis one, two . . . [gigglegiggle]." I fumbled for the Stop button. Hooky gave me a weird look. I shrugged.

"I must have pressed Play on accident." I flipped my hair out of my face and exhaled.

He nodded slowly.

I glanced down at my notebook. It read, "begin rhyming" so I repeated that out loud, but as a question and with more verbs. I carefully pressed Record.

He talked about growing up on the block in Brooklyn back in the eighties and everyone all of a sudden discovering Doug E. Fresh, The Sugar Hill Gang, and Krs-One.

"We used to trade tapes like they was gold," he said smiling, his dreadlocks swinging from side to side. "But not tapes we recorded on a stereo 'cause nobody had that. We used to have to hold our tape recorders up to the radio and get songs from the few rap shows on the stations like Kiss FM with Red Alert and Chuck Chillout."

"Sounds like love at first listen."

He laughed and said,

"Yeah. Everyone was a graf artist or a deejay or an emcee, ciphering on the corners and trading albums so that's what I wanted to be . . . an emcee."

"I see." This wasn't going as bad as I thought. Actually, it was more like a conversation where I tried not to talk about myself too much.

Hooky went on to discuss his breakout cameo on another Brooklyn rapper's classic album.

"Sometimes sixteen bars is all a brutha needs," he said, kind of cocky but I liked it. It really was a nice verse so why would I argue?

I held the mini-cassette recorder in between us, my hand was still shaking and I hoped he didn't notice. He ruminated about his family (absent West Indian father) and future on the road and in Europe touring for the next year to promote the album. He seemed like a kindhearted, serious, very high guy who'd be determined in his youth to successfully tell his story and break out of the gutter. He stared at my lips when I asked him questions.

After about ten minutes or so, I heard heavy footsteps clunking down the hall. I looked over Hooky's shoulder into the doorway and saw Noah's face come into the light. He tilted his head back a little, as though he was checking in on me. I raised my eyebrows and smiled. He nodded back, paused and then turned back into the darkness. It made me happy he'd come by.

After I asked Hooky about his change in styles on his new album and his feelings on being compared to Talib Kweli, he answered openly:

"I'm frustrated and tired of labels and of being pitted against other emcees."

I countered with, "Hip-hop always loved a good battle."

"Yeah, but it's like you gotta be a poor underground emcee, talkin' about politics and racism and all that serious shit and if you go out for cheddar and make a club banger, I sold out," he pounded his chest. "Maybe I want a Timbaland beat. Maybe I like Timbaland. Maybe I got kids to feed and clothe. I ain't here to save the world." He was out of breath when he finished the tirade.

I felt like I was losing control of this interview.

"I guess people feel comfortable labeling others," I said. "It's lazy."

He just shrugged and slowly, rather menacingly said, "Labels are dangerous."

I thought the THC might be having an adverse, paranoid effect and I'd gotten all the quotes I needed for my story, so we wrapped up our convo with a firm handshake and a mutual thank you. When I did make it (marching slowly) back to the family room, Noah was sitting in the corner and waved my way.

He rose in front of me and yanked up the sleeves on his tan, cable-knit sweater. He had a giant cross tattoo on one forearm with the name "Jessica 1980–1997" written in script underneath. He noticed me reading it.

"My sister," he said, putting his hand over the words.

"Oh," I said, shocked. "That must be hard."

He nodded.

"Anyway, it's nice to see you, Sophie. I peeped your name on the studio roster." He kissed me on the cheek and hugged me tight. His kiss actually landed on the corner of my mouth.

"You too," I said over his shoulder, tapping his back.

He sighed.

"So, how are you?" he asked, stepping back.

"I'm good." I strained for conversation.

"Yeah well, you look good," he said smiling wider.

"I do?" I looked down at my feet. "Thanks." I touched his arm.

In a case of guilt by association, charming thoughts of Jack immediately flooded my mind, swimming the butterfly stroke and racking up the laps. Why was it so hard to remember why I hated him? Why was I so lovesick? I knew I'd eventually have to pry Noah for official confirmation on Jack's dating status with you-know-who, but I'd need to be slick about it and not cause a big splash.

"You know Furious, right?" Noah asked.

I hadn't heard that name in a bit.

"Yeah, I haven't talked to him in a long time."

"He's in the A Room right now, recording with Spice."

I saw the cute freckle guy pass by us in the corridor and glance quickly our way.

"Oh, well, see, I don't know how much Furious would want to see me."

"I just popped in and told him you were here and he said you were his homegirl."

Me? His homegirl? Something was fishy, I could sense it.

"C'mon, he's a cool guy." Noah grabbed my wrist and led me through the dim light to the door. I could feel the roughness of his calloused hands scratching my skin. Jack had told me Noah played the drums.

Before we could knock, Furious opened the door.

"Hey, ma." He embraced me.

I hugged him back.

"I'm sorry," fell out of my mouth.

"That's water under the bridge now. Plus," he reached over and gave Noah a pound, "this is my man."

"Landmark seems to be a small world," I said. I peeked through the doorway and saw the back of Spice's head mixing over the boards.

"I'm on the clock," Furious said, looking at his Jacob the Jeweler watch.

"No sweat, man," said Noah. "Just wanted to say whaddup."

Furious smiled. I'd missed that smile.

"Thanks yo."

"We'll leave you alone now," I said.

"All right, babe, but I'ma call you soon and you can come check out Friday's session. We're getting Tony Loca to come in and freestyle in the booth with Mela and Tre. Noah here's working the session." He patted Noah's back.

I didn't know half those names, but it sounded like Furious and his career were doing just fine without me.

"Sounds tight," I said, hugging him bye.

Furious shut the door and Noah and I made our way back to the den. He slid his arm around my neck as we walked.

"So, have you talked to my man Jack?" he asked.

I turned to him and grit my teeth.

"I wouldn't exactly put it that way," I said, recalling the morning hang-up, air escaping from my mouth in a whistle.

bent

Later that Landmark night, Lucy and I sashayed over to the album release party for Storm, a hardcore rap group from the gutter of Lefrak, Queens. The celebration was being held at Bailar, a Latino dance club uptown. Because the group had a real ghetto rep, security was slow and thorough. I didn't care about the wait. I savored being there, hanging out and anticipating the show.

The majority of our entry was spent outside the club, in line with about a hundred grimy, randy dudes wearing leather jackets and bling-bling chains. Collectively, the hornballs wouldn't stop peeking at both me in my suede dress and Lucy, whose Anglo slimness, flame-red hair, and milky skin was now exotic. It felt like sharks were circling us, ready to chomp. I didn't want to let on to Lucy that I was growing somewhat uncomfortable (this was my new scene, after all) so I just kept smiling like a geek.

I'd brought her as my "plus one," with a temperate, almost

tempting warning that the evening was going to be a "thug fest." Anyway, she seemed to like the fringe danger in a sick, slumming on the wrong side of the tracks kind of way. I also told her that Storm had, in my opinion, made one of the best albums of that year and I'd bet some Benjamins that if their faces were prettier, they'd have a platinum album on their hands. She yawned and said "fine."

I said that instead, they'd be lucky to push 250 G's. She nodded vacantly and shifted her feet. Suddenly, a tall kind of dorky-looking boy with specs said,

"You ladies like hip-hop?"

I smiled. Lucy rolled her eyes.

" 'Cause I'm a emcee," he said, evoking the male "just keep talking" technique. I recognized him from Furious's Open Mic Night. So did that mean Furious might be here? I peered over the crowd but didn't see him.

I decided to play dumb with him to pass the time.

"You're a rapper, really?"

He stepped back.

"Hell yeah, I host this Open Mic Night on the Bowery."

"Wow," I said, nudging Lucy.

"That's so caliente," she purred.

"We don't know very much about rap music," I said. "Maybe you can teach us later." I winked.

Suddenly, we heard a bouncer call us from the front of the line.

"You two!"

"Us?" I asked.

He was pointing our way.

"Yeah," he smiled. "Get up here." He waved.

We shrugged and pushed through all the guys like the newly crowned VIPs we were, complete with some real "hello, move!" attitude. I saw the Landmark cutie on the way, and he looked at us, but in the spirit of acting special and being on edge, I pretended not to recognize him. The Open Mic guy yelled "see you inside!"

The club was, to invoke the legendary Jimi Hendrix, drenched in a purple haze. Purple from the neon lights that surrounded the square dance floor. Haze courtesy of Dutch Masters. It smelled like a four-alarm blaze. Standing at the doorway with Lucy, I felt like I was in a eighties music video, silhouetted by the white light seeping through the archway. Maybe, I should break out some kind of grand Broadway dance step, throw up the Fosse jazz hands, I thought. Maybe not.

A mass of people converged by the bar on the right side. We gravitated toward them.

It was packed with even more guys than on the line (like four to one ratio in favor of the females). We moved in deeper. Guys were clinging to their plastic cups. Were we at a Michigan kegger? No, I figured the glass bottles must have been too much a hazard. Easily transformed into a weapon.

I was pulling on my suede FUBU dress to smooth it down over my tummy pooch. My gold bangle bracelets were sliding up and down my arm. I had my pricey peekaboo red pumps on. They made me stand up straight and have nice posture.

Lucy looked fantastic though, in her black leather pants with stars stitched down the side and a white tank top. She looked like a motorcycle mama.

"Guys love me in these pants and I don't know why," she said, sliding her hand down her thigh.

"They make you look wild," I said. "And maybe they associate that with being wild in bed." I shrugged.

Lucy laughed.

"I wasn't really looking for an exact reason, but thanks, Sophie." She touched my arm in that "it'll be okay," condescending way.

I hated when my friends—who all knew that I'd never had sex—treated me like some little lamb or newborn baby. Like I had no idea what was going on in the world because I was a virgin.

I needed a drink. Or like, three of them.

"Let's get a beer," I said. Lucy nodded. We pushed through the crowd.

It was an alarmingly large number of well-groomed men—Asian, black, and Latino men mostly—dressed in black slacks, collared shirts, and black leather jackets. And other rougher, scruffier guys (the ones I was more attracted to) in jeans and sweaters and Timberlands. A lot of Avirex. I eyed one of them, chocolate skin and big black eyes, smoking a cigarette, holding it in between his index and thumb finger in a dangerous "Scarface" way. I literally felt my face flush. He watched me and Lucy pass by.

"I love this song," I said.

"Who is it?" she asked.

"M.O.P. 'Ante Up,'" I said.

We waved to get the bartender's attention and I glanced down the bar at a gorgeous woman with long dark hair and the biggest boobs I'd ever seen. As she talked to a man on her side, she leaned on the bar and sort of framed her chest with her arms. I wanted to be that alluring.

"What can I get you?" the bartender asked.

"What's free?" Lucy asked.

"Heineken and Remy Martin."

I went with beer and Lucy took the cognac.

"Wanna dance?" I asked. I wasn't in the mood to talk all night.

"Sure," she said.

We went smack-dab in the middle of the floor. There were two couples grinding next to us, lost in their own sexy worlds. The deejay announced the last song before the opening act came on. It was Pharoahe Monch's "Simon Says." The crowd cheered, jumping up and down to the chorus. I pictured Jack for a second, dancing by himself at that party, but then I pushed the thought of him away.

Lucy was doing the same dance she always did—a cute kind of waist shimmy with one hand snapping fingers, the other waving her drink side to side. My usual, she once informed me, had a lot to do with shaking my butt and doing a wavy thing with my arms.

"What's so funny?" She screamed in my ear, still dancing, not missing a beat.

I shook my head.

"I just interviewed this guy," I screamed back, pointing my finger upward to the voice surrounding us.

"Cool," she mouthed and swirled around.

It was one of those moments where I actually could feel how

much fun I was having. I spun around and felt dizzy with glorious nightlife freedom—the right to party, as the Beasties would say.

When the song ended, Lucy and I moved to a barely lit corner off the dance floor. The crew was setting up the opening act when one dude went and placed a banner in front of the deejay stand. As he unrolled it, I read the name "Furious," scribbled in supersize graffiti script.

"No way," I said out loud.

"What?" Lucy asked. There were tiny sweat beads on her brow from dancing.

"That's my friend. He's performing, I guess."

"Is that bad?"

I shook my head.

"No. I'm just surprised is all."

The crowd gathered in front of the stage and within minutes Furious took over. His dreadlocked deejay rallied the crowd.

"Give it up for my man," the deejay yelled, "he's the next big thing!"

The crowd screamed and hollered. Lucy and I clapped. Furious grabbed the mic, went to the center of the stage and launched into a song. He took off like a rocket up there, pumping his fist, running from one side of the stage to the other, freestylin' and basically owning the mic. He gave a shout out to Storm at the end of his set, someone threw him a white towel and as he made his way thru the crowd, people congratulated him with hand slaps, pats on the back and pounds. I overheard one girl calling him "a hottie."

I stood in front of him and he smiled.

"Nice set," I yelled in his ear.

"Thanks, babe," he said, hugging me. A bodyguard started to pull him in another direction.

"Furious, we gotta go," the burly man said.

Furious turned to me.

"I'll be back," he said.

Furious kept his promise and came to find me not fifteen minutes later. He was carrying a drink for me, which I shared with Lucy.

"I don't think we've met before," Furious said, taking Lucy's hand.

She shook her head.

"Great show," she said.

He kissed her hand.

Moments later, Lucy was sitting on a couch and Furious and I were in our own world, evaluating the merits of a currently circulating rumor about a (maybe) closeted rapper (also known in the industry as the "Which Rappers Are Gay" debate). We were getting heated over one old school Pittsburgh rapper in particular when Storm took the stage with about twenty of their closest friends from around the way. Not surprisingly, the performance quickly turned hectic.

"Yo, folks have to clear the stage. I'm dead ass, yo," shouted one of the members, pacing in front of the crowd.

"You know," I said turning to Furious and pointing my finger, "every time I've seen them live, they have like half their block performing with them. And each time they play, they say the same thing about it. So what the hell?"

He raised his eyebrows and laughed.

"I can't believe you worked at *Boldly Beautiful,* Sophie. I like that you ain't easy to read. Challenging."

From where we stood, that job seemed like a lifetime ago.

"So are you," I said. "I read your *BeatMaker* bio that said you graduated college." I put my hand over my mouth.

"Yeah. I went to the School of Hard Knocks."

"Seriously," I said.

"What? I can't be edjamacated?"

I laughed.

"It's cool that you did it," I said.

"I wanted to get my business degree but I didn't make it that far."

"Ah well," I sighed. "Your backup career as a rapper seems to be working out nicely."

He nodded.

"I'm so blessed. Did I tell you me and Moms moved?"

I shook my head.

"Oh, you gotta come out and see the place. It's da bomb."

"So you're all bougie now?"

"We're flossin'." He smiled. "Me and Mom. I bought her a Cadillac too."

"Wow, that advance must have been pretty nice."

"Yeah. Now I just gotta pay it all back."

"That's the rub," I nodded. "You'll get there," I said, touching his wrist.

He gave me the eyes. You know, *the eyes.*

I shuddered.

"I want to go back though," he said.

I snapped out of my head.

"Where? To the bar?" I asked, pointing across the room.

"No, to college. To get my MBA someday. Hello."

He knocked on my head.

"Oh right, I'm sorry. I spaced out for a second."

"Do you want another drink?" Furious asked, looking down at my plastic cup.

I shrugged. It was kind of fun to be distracted and stupid and careless. To get bent.

"I'll be right back," I said to Lucy. She gave me a thumbs-up.

"Come with me," Furious said grabbing my wrist as we beelined for the bar. People moved out of our way when we approached. Guys gave him pounds and said stuff like "that was dope, man" and some of the ladies out and out winked at him. I could never be that bold.

We pushed behind some random, rowdy people. I estimated the crowd holding at about two-thirds men. It was getting to that time of the night where they'd start desperately hitting on every girl relentlessly. The mass parted when they saw me and my semi-famous friend heading their way.

"What do you want?" Furious asked, leaning over the bar.

"Just another beer is cool . . . a Heineken, thanks."

I felt people moving behind me, rubbing up against my back, a stray elbow poking me here and there. Furious and I went back to Lucy.

"It was funny seeing you up at Landmark," he said.

We clinked our plastic cups together. Lucy went to the bathroom.

"Weird, eh?"

"Yeah, you're like Little Miss Hip-Hop now."

"I guess you created a monster."

He laughed and rubbed my shoulder.

"I'm proud of you," he said.

Success agreed with Furious, making his eyes twinkle and my heart race.

"Do you like recording up at Landmark?"

He shrugged.

"Yeah, it's aight. The equipment is old school, so you get that real gully New York street vibe. The cats are cool . . . Noah, Tyran—good peeps. Noah's a dope engineer."

He guzzled his beer from the plastic cup and ended up with, I'm not kidding you, one of those frosted mustaches that you only see on commercials. It was too cute to wipe.

"And what, in your expert opinion, makes a great engineer?" I sipped my beer.

He lit a cigarette and said, "A dope engineer will always keep the tape rolling." He exhaled, dipped his hand back slightly and cracked a slow smile.

I nodded and told myself to remember the sound advice. We paused and the group launched into their first single, "Trees," an homage to smoking weed. The hook of the song chopped from an ambulance siren.

Furious licked his upper lip and turned to me again. I noticed that up close, his eyes were really yellow-flecked brown, like a wildflower.

"You're gonna have to come by and see my new crib," he said, sliding his arm around my neck.

"Thanks for the invite. Maybe I'll take you up on it sometime," I said, looking into my cup where a Furious ash was floating.

Lucy leaned over my shoulder.

"I'm leaving," she said.

"Crap." I turned around. "I'm so sorry . . ." *I totally forgot you.*

"No, don't sweat it, he's pretty cute," she whispered in my ear.

"He's cute," I repeated.

"I know, I just said that," Lucy answered.

"Does he seem nice?" I asked, probably louder than was discreet.

She shrugged.

"Sure. I'm just really fucked up so I should go home."

"Don't leave," I said. "We're having fun."

"I can't stay, babe. I'm turning into the third wheel. Be safe," she kissed me on the cheek and poof, disappeared.

I turned back to him. Both of him.

The next thing I knew Furious and I were couple dancing to "Beat Down His Ass," "Fuck Yo' Mama," and other romantic hardcore rap classics. My hands were interlaced around Furious's neck and his arms enveloped my waist. The lights in the club kept blinking on and off, but we kept swaying undisturbed like two young lovebirds in a middle school gym swooning to "Careless Whispers."

I wondered if Noah was around, maybe behind us in the crowd? Or any *BeatMaker* staffers? I didn't want to know. Folks around us seemed to be pumping their fists in slow-mo. We twirled.

At one point, my feet were hurting so bad from my cute, ridiculously painful shoes that I told Furious I had to sit down.

We went to a couch in the back corner. The couch had nasty

stains all over it, but I was too buzzed to care. We sat in the middle and I leaned onto his shoulder.

"Let me take those off for you," he said, undoing the fastens and carefully removing my shoes.

When he was done treating me like Cinderella, I tucked my throbbing feet under my legs.

"You all right?" he asked.

"Sure," I nodded. "Just sleepy is all."

"Let me get you a cab. It's late."

We walked out and Furious grabbed my hand. We passed Kevin, Landmark's owner, by the exit and he flashed me this look of total disbelief.

On the curb, Furious stood with his arm out as all these cabbies drove by.

He came back over to me.

"You might wanna try," he said. "Taxi drivers don't really stop for black men. Especially at 2 a.m."

Something about what he said and how he said it, all slowly and matter-of-fact made me want to give him the biggest kiss of my life. So that's just what I did.

His lips were soft and inviting. He gripped my waist.

"Damn, Sophie. I wasn't expecting *that*."

I went to punch his arm playfully, missed, lost my balance and went tumbling off the curb. He reached out to catch me.

"Whoa," I laughed. "I almost fell." I couldn't stop laughing.

"Almost," he said. "But I caught ya." He shook his head.

"I should go now," I said and walked toward the oncoming traffic. He held my hand so I wouldn't wander right into the cars.

I hailed the next cab.

"Never fails," he said, shaking his head.

I turned to say good-bye.

"I'll call you tomorrow, Sophie. Get home safe."

He pecked my lips and I hopped in. I looked back at him as I drove away and waved.

The next morning was a different children's story. The harsh light of day (and my cell) zapped me back to life. I climbed out of the bed, crawled to my purse and retrieved my phone. My head soon followed.

Last night with Furious had been a dream, right?

I flipped open my phone. It was Fred from the office. My heart was thumping.

"HP is sick so I need you to fill in for his Slick Rick interview," he said.

"Okay," I said still in a haze. I was lying with my head at the foot of my bed, massaging my temples.

"Cool," he said.

"Just one thing," I said, squinting from the strong a.m. sunlight.

"Shoot."

"Did you just say 'Slick Rick'?"

"Yeah," he said chuckling.

"Slick Rick the Ruler?" I asked. My mouth was parched, and my voice was hoarse, so it took great effort to get that out.

"That's the one. Did you have a rough night or something?"

"Did I?" I wondered. Then it hit me. "I'm interviewing Slick Freaking Rick!" I squealed into the phone.

"Okay, Sophie, chill out. Don't get too psyched," Fred said.

"Oh," I said sitting back down, "I'm totally not. I'll hold it down."

"We've got an exclusive but it's a phoner."

That meant Mr. Rick and I wouldn't be meeting vis-à-vis. Blah! I probably should've acted professional and hid being let down but instead I made an unpleasant noise that sounded something like a pirate going "arghhhhhhhh." Fred ignored my infantile grumble.

"Your call in time is eleven, so if you want to do it from home and then come into the office afterward that's fine."

I glanced at the time on my cell: 10:07 a.m.

"Yeah, sounds good. I got this, don't sweat it."

"Check your BlackBerry for the details."

I hardly knew how to work that stupid text-messaging contraption.

"You got it," I said.

I could hear Fred having a hearty laugh on the other end of the line. "What's so funny now?" I asked.

"Smith saw you up at the Storm party last night and's been telling everybody you were slow dancing with . . ."

"Furious?" I asked, vaguely remembering our hookup.

Smith loved to rag on me. It felt like some hazing ritual he was putting me through.

"Yeah, right," I said, blowing off the info. "Tell Smith to mind his own business and stop trying to ruin my game."

"Sophie's wild, yo!" I heard Smith yell in the background. "We got the photos to prove it!"

I couldn't put two and two together to save my life.

"I am whatever you say I am," I said, quoting Eminem.

"Hey, it's between you all," Fred said.

I heard Smith say, "Industry guys are strictly hit-it and quit-it," but Fred didn't acknowledge his statement.

"Good luck with Rick. Peace, Sophie."

I put my phone down shell-shocked, but I had little time to recreate the events and piece together the timeline of last night. I was highly discombobulated, fog-headed, and I had less than forty-three minutes to get my shit together.

I grabbed the pink floral towel hanging on my doorknob and hit the shower.

While the almost scalding hot water drizzled all over me, I thought of Furious. For some reason I was remembering him much more affectionately than platonically. And then, it came: the kiss outside the club. The Kiss. The smell of sweet cologne and cigarette smoke. The bend of our necks. Skin meeting. It was intoxicating to think about. Exciting. New.

I let my imagination have a big, summertime holiday: I pictured me and Furious dating and me meeting his mom in his new, fancy house. I pictured all that *space* in the house. I imagined myself going to Landmark to meet him after a recording session and playing video games with him in the rec room to chill out. I saw us escaping from New York together for a weekend and playing cards in Atlantic City, then zooming for sun on the Jersey shore.

I dreamed of him making me pancakes in his pajama pants while I made him laugh from the bed. Of him writing raps about me. Me hanging backstage. I dreamed of us as a couple, taking over the hip-hop world together. Like Russell and Kimora. Puff and J-Lo. Meth and Mary.

By the time I returned from never-never land, my fingertips looked like raisins and I'd washed my hair three times. I'd spent enough time this morning on my dreams for the future and another more present one was about to explode through my telephone. So, I stepped out of the hot steam, wiped myself down with a towel, and mentally checked off my questions for Slick Rick. Questions I'd been wanting to ask him years ago after hearing "Mona Lisa" for the first time.

Throughout the interview and the train ride to work, I'd managed to replace my thoughts of Furious with the afterglow of Slick Rick talking to me. ME! He'd even said my name a couple of times! Things were all good—that is, until I got to work.

When I was walking the hallway to my desk, I was getting a *really* weird vibe from everyone. I tapped on Amon's glass window and he turned around and he just gave me this look like "yikes." Most people were just facing their computers and deliberately ignoring my presence. Then Jenna and her tupperware box bumped into me.

"Sophie," she said. "Whoa."

"Whoa?" I asked, totally confused. "What?"

"Uhhh," she said, pointing to the microwave in the kitchen. "I gotta go."

I shook my head and stopped by Fred's office on the way to my desk. It felt like I'd entered another dimension. I knocked and peered inside. He looked up from some blue lines he was going over.

"Slick Rick went well," I said, leaning in.

He nodded.

"Don't be mad at me," he clapped his hands together.

"I'm not. Should I be?" I asked, moving into his office. I chewed on the ends of my hair.

"Have you seen *BeatMaker*'s Web site today?"

I shook my head.

"No, I came in right after the phoner and just got here," I said, touching my vintage Gucci bag with crumbled papers creeping out.

"Shut the door," he said. "And come over here."

He swiveled his chair toward his computer. I walked over to him and looked over his shoulder. He clicked through the homepage and then onto our gossip column. Suddenly, a large, full-screen photo of me and Furious came up.

There we were dancing at last night's party! I looked cross-eyed! Furious had his arms around me! Fuckshitfuck!

I stepped away.

"Oh. My. God." I felt my toes and fingers go cold. I went back over Fred's shoulder. He hadn't turned around to face me. I read the photo caption. "*BeatMaker*'s own Sophie Drakas getting to know MC Furious at the Storm album release party."

"I feel like I'm going to puke," I told Fred, touching my stomach.

He spun around.

"Don't. It's really not that bad," he said, nibbling the end of his pen.

I put my hands on my hips and leaned back against the wall.

"Really, how do you figure?"

"Well, just try to see it as one of those night-out paparazzi shots they put in the back of magazines." He forced a smile.

"Fred, I look like a lush. Like a chickenhead," I pointed at the screen. "I can't believe it," I sighed, hiding my face in my hands. I felt like I was going to erupt into big, salty tears, but then what came out of me was a burst of uncontrollable giggles. I looked at Fred and could not stop laughing. My eyes watered, my belly ached, I actually *snorted.*

"Okay then," he said. "That's better." He patted my shoulder.

"Well," I said, standing up and tucking in my shirt, "sometimes you either gotta laugh or cry. Today, why the hell not enjoy the absurdity. Right?"

He nodded.

"If you want, go tell Smith I said take it down."

"Thanks, Fred."

I hoisted my bag over my shoulder and left his office. I could not wait to see Smith. Not surprisingly, he was less than psyched to see me.

"Yo, Sophie. Don't shoot!" He held his hands up in to shield his face.

I stepped into his cubicle. I knew the best way to play Smith was to flaunt how undisturbed and unaffected I was by his childish reindeer games.

"Why would I?" I asked.

He pulled his skully down tighter over his head and dropped his hands.

"You mean, you ain't mad?"

I twirled the ends of my hair and took my time answering.

"I can't be. I laughed my ass off. You get props for that. However, Fred does want you to pull the picture."

"That's it?" he asked, skeptically.

"Yeah, that's it."

"You know what, Sophie? You're all right for a girl." He tapped my shoulder.

I faked a smile and sprinted away, holding all my embarrassment and humiliation in, blaming myself for the dancing misstep.

droppin' dime

The next day I had to be at work at 9 a.m. sharp for an editorial meeting to discuss our annual "Notes from the Underground" issue. I actually got to work an hour before the meeting because I couldn't sleep, so I savored some strong Spanish coffee at my desk and brainstormed angles and intros to my "Drop Dime" story.

In hip-hop, droppin' dime means to rat someone out. In my article, it also meant connecting the catchy phrase with my own experiences of betrayal. After fifteen minutes of typing, this is what I'd come up with:

> The lifelong practice of the bitch-snitch seems to develop during the playground years, somewhere in-between the monkey bars and swings. The first time I snitched on someone was partly mischievous and wholly satisfying.
>
> It was back when I was in elementary school outside Detroit.

Anatomy Test time. I was a *scholarship* kid, Kelly was a rich girl who constantly teased me for wearing bargain clothes.

The night before the test, I'd labored tirelessly memorizing the femur, parietal bone, and even managing to stomach those odd sketches of 'penis' and then, when I was confidently filling out my answers, I caught Kelly peeking over my shoulder. I marched up in my Kmart shoes to Ms. Emery and whispered to her that Kelly was cheating.

For punishment, she had to stay after school with all the poor latchkey kids she hated. And, I realized snitching was totally awesome. With one major exception: when you're the one exposed.

In hip-hop, treachery is even uglier. Consummate examples include Jay-Z blasting Prodigy at a concert by displaying a photo of the QB rapper as a shorty dressed in a ballet tutu. The song "Dre Day," where the self-titled emcee calls out Ice Cube and Eazy-E, as well as refers to Luke's mama as "a Frisco dyke."

The list is seemingly endless. So many dimes dropping on and off wax, dollars start adding up—and all at someone else's expense. A costly venture.

I was feelin' it. But would my editor like it?

Rosalinda, my always hungry desk neighbor, sauntered in with a bag of Krispy Kremes and an orange juice.

I zoned out on my screen and decided to kill the next few free minutes by downloading beats by Krush and Shadow, Kid Koala and Qbert, pulses that sounded like soft sneezes and intense rainstorms.

My phone flashed and an unfamiliar number appeared. I slipped off my headphones. It was Jack. I asked him to hold and then hollered at our new Dominican intern to please turn down his Ja Rule thug ballad.

Why the hell was Jack calling me at work and why was the sound of his frail, mildly sleazy voice immediately able to level me? I sipped my lukewarm coffee and clicked back.

"What's happenin'?" I asked, gaining composure.

"I'd like to ask you the same thing," he answered flatly.

"Oh, really? Okay," I forced a laugh.

He was silent for a moment.

"I need to talk to you about something."

"Now?" I asked.

"No, let's meet," he said. "Tonight, after work, bOb bar."

"Sure," I whispered, bewildered beyond belief. Could he and Jenny have split up?

"Bye, Sophie," he said, sounding disappointed.

I didn't get a good feeling after hanging up. The intern turned Ja back up. Everyone was at work now, shuffling papers, playing music, shouting at each other.

I immediately regretted agreeing to see Jack. I was such a sucker! I slipped my headphones back on and let the beats distract me. I wanted to get swallowed up by the music, disappear completely, and escape into those sounds. *Tonight a deejay saved my life.* Instead of escaping, it was time for the Ed meeting. I printed out my intro to read in the meeting and tried to suck up my personal problems. Thing was, I couldn't distinguish my personal life from my professional life anymore.

That unseasonably sunny afternoon, I was set to follow around New Moon, an up-and-coming emcee, for part one of a story comparing the varied, daily struggles that a mainstream versus an underground hip-hop artist faces daily. "Struggles" not of the third-world country variety, but still.

New Moon was a lanky nineteen-year-old rapper/b-boy from Greenwich who produced all his own music from a makeshift studio in his parents' basement. He had dark, curly brown hair, big blue eyes and a warm complexion. During my research, one article mentioned NM was of Sephardic Orthodox Jewish descent, which was interesting to me. Something to delve into. A rich backstory to uncover and cut through the publicity B.S.

He'd seen surprising success online through his Web site and was now supposedly talking to the major labels whose attention he seemed to have cultivated methodically. So, was an ego-trippin' emcee with lyrics such as "do-or-die underground/ain't nothing to fight for up above," agreeing to sell out for the right price? Guess it wouldn't be the first time.

New Moon wanted to meet up at Fat Beats, a Village record store, to dig through some crates. Of course, in the ongoing tradition of rappers being late, he was running fifteen minutes behind. I stood by the organic pharmacy and waited. The time lapse produced banal thoughts ranging from "I could go for some French fries" to, while peeking in the Rx window, "holy shit, what's a coffee enema," (which I actually said out loud).

Being so near to NYU got me thinking about Ann Arbor and being there on those skinny streets and slinging mud at the café (where we used our coffee like normal people) and the one day I decided music was the third thing I loved most.

Before I knew it, I'd created a fresh, tiny New York world, where music, and specifically hip-hop inspired me, challenged me, tired me. It lived.

A sweaty, dark-skinned boy with big, bony knees was blasting Mobb Deep's "Shook Ones" on his boom box. We both mouthed the sly, visceral chorus. Was hip-hop really everywhere or was it just that now, I was always looking for it?

When my interviewee finally showed up the first thing mister smooth guy (even more handsome in person than in pictures) said to me was:

"You have my mom's eyes."

We shook hands. Thankfully, he had a firm shake.

"Really? I'll give 'em back to her if this interview goes well."

"I'm sorry I'm late," he said, letting me go first through the door. He was carrying a dense looking vinyl bag that weighed down his shoulder and wearing a broken-in blue Wu-Tang tour T-shirt.

"It's okay, I forgive you," I said. "Part of my job is waiting around for rappers."

He smiled and I turned on my micro-cassette recorder as we ascended the one flight of stairs.

"Are we on the record now?" he asked holding the heavily stickered and marked up door to the store open when we'd reached the top.

"On the record," I nodded, passing through. "No pun intended," I said, moving to a row of albums.

He shuffled to a corner and I followed. The store looked like a giant box decorated in bright hip-hop posters, with a couple guys in baseball caps and saggy jeans loafing around, leaning over crates, plucking more squares.

There were a few random backpacks discarded on the floor and Bill Withers playing in the background. One clerk stood behind an elevated checkout area, in front of the only CDs for sale. He was Asian and hardly looked up from the video game magazine he was perusing to acknowledge us.

"Just make me look good," he said.

"I'll try," I answered, moving to his side.

While we wove in between the rows of music, I couldn't help but think of Jack. The thought that I would be seeing him a few hours thrilled me. New Moon didn't seem to vibe my mental vacation. He just kept talking. And talking. And talking.

I flipped my tape over to the other side.

"I'ma kick this new joint I wrote for you. It's titled 'Like A House' and it's got all these fresh metaphors in it," he said.

"You probably mean 'similes,' " I said, trying to clear up a common linguistic misunderstanding with rappers.

"Whatever, smarty. Let's just get the fuck out of here, eh? There's a Gray's Papaya on the corner and I'm hella starved," he slapped me on the back.

"I don't eat meat, but okay. It's your day, after all." I followed him down the stairs, hoping a hot dog would quiet him.

That night I went to the bar to meet Jack. I picked a corner table and checked my fuchsia lipstick about ten million times in my compact, as minutes slowly ticked down. After about an hour of waiting for him and no cell number to reach him at, I left a message on his home phone letting him know his passive-aggressive shit was really hurtful and confusing.

Then I went home to my bedroom and played some Bob Marley fight music to christen my own revolution and, like Tupac, keep my head up.

In the middle of the night, I was awoken to my phone blaring in the other room. I went to it like a zombie in the dark.

"Hello," I said, standing in my kitchenette with the lights out and the phone pressed to my ear.

"Sophie, it's Jack."

"Lucky me," I said.

"I see your wit is still intact," he said.

"It's 4 a.m., Moretti, and you blew me off tonight."

"I know. I'm sorry. I punked out."

"What's really up?"

"Noah told me about Furious."

"So?" I asked, moving to lay on the couch, rubbing my toes together once I got there.

"Just watch out, you know. He's got a rep for being a player. I mean, he *is* a rapper."

"Thanks for the newsflash."

"C'mon, Sophie. I'm just trying to warn you."

"What do you care?"

"I do. I really do. A lot."

"I think you should go worry about Jenny and just leave me alone."

He sighed.

"Fine," he said. "Have it your way."

"Good night, Jack."

"Take care," he said.

"I will."

shook ones

The next night I was headed to Furious's East Orange, NJ, digs in a car service Lincoln Continental that he'd ordered for me. I was feeling excited to see his new place and felt grateful that he'd taken care that I could. Marvin Gaye's "Sexual Healing" came on the radio and the driver turned the tune up.

I felt such a release getting out of the city—seeing trees and a glimpse of the horizon even. As we approached East Orange, the farms and windy roads reminded me of the terrain in Michigan, except with more hills.

I tapped my foot along and mouthed the words to the song. I was wearing a pea coat and a jean skirt with knee-high leather boots, and the backs of my bare thighs were sticking to the vinyl seat. I supposed I deserved the uncomfort for trying to look sexy in winter. I was dressed in between seasons and actually, that's how I felt inside. Like something was turning in me.

We pulled up to a long, curvy driveway where a two-story house was awaiting at the top of the incline. Suddenly, I became so nervous that my stomach cramped up. I took a couple deep breaths as we got closer to the entranceway. I took out my compact and smoothed on some powder. I cracked my knuckles. I'd hung out with Furious so many times before, but this experience was instantly different, on a foreign plain, in another language almost.

The driver came around to open the door, and when I stepped outside, I noticed the sun setting and lingering in the sky. The cold air smelled fresh and snapped me alive.

"Thanks," I said to the driver. He touched his leather cap to acknowledge me, got back in the Lincoln and pulled away.

I walked up the steps. There was a Christmas wreath on the door, with candy canes and tree cones attached to the pine needles. Someone had also woven plastic little microphones into the circle. I rang the bell and saw an obscured body approaching.

The door opened and a smiling, chubby black lady with big dark curls falling around her face and the most luminous and creamy skin I'd ever seen appeared. She was one of those people who could be forty or sixty. Age was unable to mark her. Instantly, I felt at ease in her peaceful presence.

"Welcome," she said, holding the door open for me.

"Hello," I said, shaking her hand but she stopped me.

"Oh, give me a hug, honey," she said, leaning into me. "I'm Bernice, Earnest's mama."

Earnest?

"I'm Sophie. Very nice to meet you," I said, following her into the house.

"I know who you are," she laughed.

It was grand inside—all cream-colored carpeting and beige leather couches and a staircase with a wooden banister that seemed to lead up to the clouds. There was a skylight over the hallway and it smelled like fresh potpourri had been scattered around.

"Should I take off my shoes?" I asked.

"You don't have to," she said.

We walked down the hall, passing by framed black-and-white photos of musical greats—Coltrane, Miles, Jimi—and into a huge kitchen with gray tile and granite and a Viking range and a Sub Zero fridge. French windows opened up the room onto the expansive backyard where a light snow had dusted the ground.

Furious's mom went and stood behind the island. There was a huge crystal vase in front of me, holding a massive number of freshly bloomed red roses.

"Have a seat, baby," she said.

I took a stool facing her, inhaling the flowery scent wafting around us. A pink hue from the sunset was reflecting in the room.

"Earnest's running a little late from the studio."

"No worries," I said, resting my purse on the next stool.

"Let me make you something to eat until he gets here."

My first thought was to be polite and say No. But my second, smarter thought was I bet this woman can cook.

"Sure, if it's not a problem. I'll try something."

She went to the fridge and heaved open the stainless steel doors.

"We got some leftover yellow squash risotto, some fried chicken, a beet-and-spinach salad, and I can heat up some macaroni and cheese."

My tongue tingled and my taste buds stood at attention.

"Some mac-n-cheese and salad sounds delicious."

"All right then," she said, her back still to me as she went digging in the fridge for certain Tupperware boxes and other dishes.

She crossed to turn on the oven.

"I never use the microwave," she said. "Maybe I'm old-fashioned. That's what Earnest calls me."

She put the mac-n-cheese in the oven and emptied the salad into a clear bowl.

"Your house is gorgeous," I said.

"Thank you," she said, pouring me a tall glass of water. "You know my boy has been working really hard for a lot of years. He always told his mama that he'd buy her a house someday and I thank the Lord every day for these blessings." She looked up to heaven, so I did too. Another skylight.

"Yeah, it's a beautiful thing," I said, admiring the high, vaulted ceiling.

"For years it was always just me and Earnest in one bedroom apartment on Grand Concourse. He sleeping on the couch, we barely scraping by, but I prayed and prayed."

Just then, the front door squeaked open.

"I'm home," a voice yelled from the foyer. Furious. "Is Sophie here?"

"Yes," I hollered.

Bernice smiled.

"Hey, Mama," he said, coming in and kissing her on the cheek.

"Hey, Sophie," he said, coming over and laying one on me.

My heart skipped a beat.

"Hey," I swallowed.

Furious grabbed a stool and his mom went and fixed us two big plates of leftovers. Afterward, Furious and I went to the basement where he'd set up a mini studio and den area. It was dank down there, smelled wet. One half a makeshift recording studio, the other half a typical male hangout spot.

I gravitated to all the CDs lining the wall. He went straight for his turntables, where crates stuffed with vinyl were hiding underneath as his auditory arsenal.

"I don't just have mic skills, Sophie," he said, snapping the fader to life. "I'm a hot deejay too."

"Really?" I said, reclining on a fluffy black velvet couch. "Prove it."

So, he spun some records—mixing Al Green with G-Unit and a dash of Quik here and there. He threw on Warren G and Nate Dogg's "Regulate" and I giggled with joy. I watched him rotate, swap and scratch each album back and forth rhythmically. He cradled the earphones on his shoulder, ducking away to hear the next song or his place on the record. It looked like he was concentrating really hard.

In those minutes, I realized that my rap affection was strongest for the deejay. I always seemed to be drawn to him—onstage and off. Maybe it was that he didn't grab the spotlight, but laid the beats that everyone nodded their heads to. Maybe it was that he often possessed an extensive knowledge of different types of music from Journey to Bessie Smith, David Bowie to John Coltrane. And then there was, if he was worth his weight or purity, a steadfast commitment to spinning strictly vinyl.

Perhaps it too was the fluid motion of him crouching down to his records, flipping through the crates as if it were second nature to pluck the perfect one. Or maybe it was the way he, like Furious, would lick the tips of his fingers before scratching a record and then precisely drop the needle on the next joint, swaying his hips to the rhythm, rotating moods, feelin' himself.

Might be that sure-thing grin that would spread across his face when the crowd reacted with a deep, collective sigh and he knew he'd gotten it just right. Then he'd nod his head all nonchalant and shit like "oh yes I did." God, I loved that.

Whatever the deejay's specific allure, it really began with a universal truism about the male species—they're hotter when they're doing something. Put an average-looking guy behind a drum set or on a sports field or touching some turntables and his hot quotient instantly doubles.

Other people had oysters and chocolate, but this was my foreplay. My aphrodisiac.

I think Furious sensed I was interested in him at that moment because he put on Shuggie Otis, dimmed the lights, and slid over next to me on the couch. He rested his head on my shoulder. My body trembled.

"You cold?" he asked, reaching for a blanket lying on the couch.

"Thanks," I said, tossing it over us.

Suddenly, we were kissing and his hands were all over me. As each piece of clothing peeled off us and our warm skin and desire and sweat was mingling under the cover, I kept thinking, wow this is actually happening. To ME! With a semi-famous rapper!

The other things I kept thinking were "I'm wearing my granny panties" and "I haven't waxed my legs for two weeks." Yuck. I tried to keep his face above my waist to divert his attention from my matronly grooming and anti-lingerie.

The next thing I knew I was totally naked. So was he. We paused.

"Is this okay?" he asked.

"Yeah," I said. Out with my pesky virginity!

He tore a condom packet open with his teeth like a wild beast and slid it over himself deftly. He climbed on top of me, there was some pokiness, a loud grunt and then, unluckily, a call from the top of the stairs:

"Earnest! Sophie! Ya'll want some coconut cream pie I just finished making?"

We looked at each other mid-thrust, bug-eyed and out of breath.

Coconut cream pie?

"Shit. Pretend like I'm tickling you," he said. His brow was glistening.

"What?" I asked, hearing a thump, thump, thump coming down the stairs. My heart raced. "I'm not ticklish."

"She's coming down," he said, throwing on his T-shirt and lifting the cover over us.

"I'm still naked," I squeaked in fear.

"Laugh," he commanded.

He tickled my belly with purpose and I let out the biggest, fakest burst of laughter I could muster. I started to wheeze from all the lung activity. My mind was spinning: granny panties, hairy legs, sex, pie.

"What did y'all say?" Mama said looking at us from the bottom of the stairs across the room.

"We ain't hungry, Mom." He smiled.

I looked at Furious frozen on top of me. He flopped down. It was actually kind of sexy to be in this moment with him. Getting caught and trying to weasel our way out of being naughty.

"Thanks though," I said, waving. I wanted to be polite and it was kind of her to offer.

She shrugged.

"Suit yourself," she said, turning to climb the stairs.

We stared at each other in silence. Nothing like a mom walking in to break the mood. I covered my mouth. Furious was making a face and trying to get me to laugh, but I was too tense. We'd dodged a bullet; a frisson of excitement and relief took over my body.

When we finally heard the door slam, Furious put his face in front of mine and held my cheeks in his hands.

"You're gorgeous," he said.

I reached up to kiss him.

"That was a real adventure, quite a ride," I said.

He laughed and lay next to me.

"We should do it again sometime," he said.

I looked up at the ceiling.

"I'veneverdoneitbefore," I coughed, smushing all the words together so he wouldn't understand.

"Say what?" he said, propping himself on his elbow and looking at me.

I saw my big, white granny panties spread on the floor. I wished I could magically wish them out of sight.

"I'm flattered," he said, his cockiness returning.

"It seemed like the right moment," I smiled. "It was definitely funnier than I thought I would be."

He nodded.

"And quicker," I laughed.

He pinched my hipbone.

"I like you, Sophie, but I wanna be straight with you."

"Only now?" I joked.

"I'm really concentrating on my music and I can't catch feelings or have a girlfriend, deal with all that."

Deal with me, he meant.

"Oh," I said. "Okay."

"But that was nice," he said as a consolation.

Whoo-fucking-hoo.

"I guess I better go," I said, not knowing what else to do. I got up with the cover and he went to fetch his boxers and jeans.

I managed to snag my underthings and keep my furry legs covered as I re-dressed.

We went upstairs, Furious called the car, his mom force-fed us pie. We ate in silence.

Everything instantly felt different—heavier, awkward, silly. The way my back curved as I sat with him on the stools, the glazed-over look in his eyes, the tone of our voices when we were parting. I kept thinking of what Jack had said on the phone, the player thing.

"I had fun," I said to Furious at the door while the Lincoln waited in the driveway.

We had sex.

"Yeah, me too," he said, putting his arms over his head and savoring a wake-up stretch.

"I'll call you later," I said, trying to neutralize the strange vibe and take control.

"Cool, babe."

He leaned in and kissed my lips in a brisk, almost perfunctory way.

I walked to the car feeling naked even though I had my clothes on. I didn't even feel empowered by getting to call him first. I felt slighted he didn't ask me to stay the night. Wonder what yumminess his Mom would be cooking up for breakfast.

"Bye," I yelled back to him.

But he'd already closed the door and gone inside.

At least I didn't have to make the Walk of Shame, I told myself for comfort as we approached Manhattan. I'd never been so happy to get home. To enter that familiar, feverish skyline. Fuck Jersey. I was 0 for 2 there.

Furious didn't return my phone call that next day or the following one. Very soon, by the third night of being ignored, I had a scary realization: exactly what I feared would happen, did. I got dissed. By a guy named EARNEST.

I checked the phone receiver on my nightstand one last time. There was a dial tone. All pathetic circuits were alive and well. I clicked the lamp off and it was pitch black. I wished I could go back in time to that night.

I had a Bahamadia phoner that next afternoon which I asked to conduct from home. It was nice to finally be interviewing a female emcee. Especially one as strong and skilled as she. *Kollage* had been one of my favorite hip-hop albums in college, not just because it grooved, because it was damn smart.

Dia was even more down-to-earth than I expected and I was more exhausted than I thought. Being wary of misconstruing my tiredness for ennui, I asked her about working with DJ Premier, raising a son, and her creative process. She came across as open, straightforward and well read, citing authors like Octavia Butler as inspiration.

So I decided to go for it.

"What's it like being a female in the cruel, cold music business?"

She laughed a deep and hearty one.

"I would think you might know."

"I want your perspective, please."

"Honestly, I don't take it all too seriously. Music is a creative outlet for me to express myself. There are a lot of shysters on the business side but usually, I try not to get wrapped up."

"You keep all that at arm's length?"

"Exactly. The dealings, the hierarchy, the male domination all stays in the background. Music is the foreground. My fans, foreground. So, I'm gonna do what I gotta do to keep balanced. I don't mix business with pleasure."

"Ah," I said, letting her words absorb into my skin. "I'm having a hard time with that."

"How old are you?"

"I'll be twenty-five soon."

"Yeah, the twenties are rough."

"How did you make it?"

"Day by day," she laughed. "And on the serious tip, just by trying not to make the same mistake twice—the second time around it ain't a mistake."

I smiled.

"It's tough working in music. There are so few women around, like to carve the way. Support you," I said.

"Yeah, it's a boys' club. And they will take advantage of you, if they can. They'll try to break you down or maybe doubt yourself or just plain get with you, but you gotta draw the line."

"You're right."

"You make the decision when to say enough or you're trippin' or you're trespassing. Don't be afraid of your power. Your female energy. Use it to your advantage."

"There's an advantage?" I asked.

"Oh yeah. You'll learn what yours is. But, my best piece of advice—especially when you're starting out—is to make rules and stick to 'em. Separate work from play."

"Yup. It's hard to get ahead in hip-hop if you're something other than a hanger-on or groupie or video ho."

"Right because people are like, 'What's she about?' They don't get you." Dia dropped her voice a couple octaves to impersonate a man's voice. " 'She's down with hip-hop?' 'She knows my songs?' 'Say what?'"

"Exactly!"

"But you gotta be persistent. Show them you're there to do your job and that's your agenda. Not to smash or hook up or be having their baby. Just work."

Oh, the irony!

"That's how you get this industry to respect you," she said. "You gotta be more brave than the dudes."

"I see."

"But like I said, you're in your twenties and making mistakes are part of growing up. You live and learn."

A click came through the line.

"Sophie, time to wrap it up," the publicist said.

"I gotta get back to grinding," Dia said.

"No problem. I really, really, really appreciate your advice."

"You're really welcome, and here's my e-mail address if you ever need to holler. Or just wanna talk."

I couldn't find any paper so I copied down the address onto my hand.

"Good luck," I said, hanging up.

"You too," she answered.

I kept the phone in my lap, savoring all the advice she'd generously doled out to little ol' me. I wasn't sure anymore if I wanted to continue my job or if I even cared enough to chance more resistance. I'd taken a big blow emotionally and didn't know when or if I'd be getting up from it.

The experience with Furious had ejected me from the land of hip-hop, ground on which I'd already struggled to find a clear path, much less a few companions.

Dia was so friendly and wise that it gave me hope all was not lost. Her music expressed that she'd been through a great deal of negativity and had come out better for it. Maybe I could too.

I worked on my story until midnight and climbed into bed feeling lonely and tired. I recalled something Lucy had recited to me from a self-help book senior year after she'd found out Evan Morrow had cheated on her with the head cheerleader. Something about living in an age of reruns, processed food, and packaged pop culture and how the one thing in society that remained wholly unpredictable and enigmatic was the possibility and experience of sleeping with someone.

The thought hadn't resonated with my naïve ears years ago, but on that night, it was the only thing that really made sense. And as I drifted away to sleep, I actually could feel myself changing because of it.

I awoke a couple hours later with the determined thought that I wanted something to change—externally. I was desperate to take back some control so I dialed Furious again. On the fourth ring, he answered.

"Yo," he said.

"Hey, what's goin' on?" My mouth went dry.

"I'm at Landmark recording. What's up?"

He sounded put-off, like I was stalking him.

"Have you been real busy?"

"I've been working a lot, yeah." He huffed.

I wanted to steer the conversation to normality. Get him to like me again. I risked it:

"I've missed you."

"Listen, I'm at work. So, let me call you back tomorrow when I get off."

"You're recording overnight?" I asked. "I could come and visit you."

"Nah, Kevin's here and I could get in trouble."

"Okay, but I want to see you soon."

"Yeah, maybe later. I gotta go, Sophie."

He hung up and the tears took over. I just felt so damn frustrated. How could I get so attached in, what was the final count? one, two, three, four, five, six minutes. I wanted to call him back and rip into him, but something told me that wouldn't make anything better.

Then a flash of inspiration came upon me: sneak up there and make *him* see *you*. I glanced at my watch. It was after two in the morning. Adrenaline kicked in.

I leapt off my bed, grabbed some suit pants and a black scoop neck sweater from my closet and raced to the bathroom. I zoomed to the kitchen and forced down a tablespoon of Pepto, gagging and applying rouge simultaneously.

I returned to the bathroom and tried to apply mascara but my hand was trembling. Instead, I just squirted some Visine into my itchy eyes. I could feel blood rushing through my veins. No more waiting around for Furious. I was taking action and in less than an hour, I'd see him and everything would be cool again. Good girl, I patted myself on the back.

I couldn't wait to give that boy a hug, hold him, smell him, touch him. The excitement was almost too much. I stuffed some tissue into my purse and hurried to turn off the lights. I didn't want to miss him in case he knocked off early. As soon as he'd see me, his anger and fear would recede, giving way to carnal desire. It had to. I had no Plan B.

I stood outside on the curb and waved down a taxi. I repeated my mantra, smoothed on some strawberry lipgloss, and licked it all off within seconds. We sped away to midtown and landed in the empty business district.

"Just drop me off here, please," I told the cabbie.

"But your stop isn't for two more blocks," he replied in a thick Ukrainian accent.

"It's fine," I said.

The car stopped, I tossed a ten spot over the seat and ejected myself just short of the Landmark door. I moved forward, looking up at the building ahead's second floor. I could see the black light shining through the window, calling me home.

At the end of the block, I came face to face with the Landmark intercom and pressed Call.

"Yeah," answered an unfamiliar, scratchy male voice on the other end.

"Hey, I'm here for Furious's session."

"You late, girl. He's wrapping up," the voice said.

"Is Noah in?" I asked.

"Yeah, he's in a session with Don Gio."

"Well, maybe I could just drop off a tape for him?"

"Who is this?"

"Sophie. From *BeatMaker*."

I heard a buzz and grabbed the door. I got to the elevator and felt so shaky. Maybe it wasn't such a good idea to surprise Furious like this. I thought of turning around and then the doors parted on floor four. It was too late.

I walked forward and looked into the bulletproof window. It was this nice guy Tyran, a coworker and buddy of Noah's, who I'd met at a recent Roc-A-Fella party. He buzzed me through and came out to the dark hallway to greet me.

"What you doing up here so late?" He gave me a squeeze.

"I was up and I forgot I promised Noah this bootleg." I knew I had no such tape in my bag so I didn't even bother pretending to look for it.

"He's in the A Room with Furious. They're mixing and recording Don Gio's new joint."

"Okay."

"It's kind of crazy up in there, so I'd just wait in the living room and Noah should be taking a break soon."

I looked over at the big screen TV, which was playing *GoodFellas.*

"It's Don's favorite movie. That guy thinks he's such a gangsta." He shook his head. "But we're just here to please." He shrugged.

"Right, right," I said. "Help create the perfect ambience for his next number one album."

"That's our motto. Anyway, I got some business in the back but I'll be out in a bit. It's finally the end of my day at . . ." he looked at his watch, "practically three a.m."

I moved closer to the common room.

"You cool?" he asked.

"Yeah, thanks," I said at the entranceway, watching Tyran walk away. As soon as he was out of sight, I crept the other direction toward the recording room. I pressed my ear to the door and heard muffled voices talking over a bass line.

I cracked the door open a bit and could see the back of Noah's neck. Furious was in the corner on a brown leather couch, gulping a can of beer and smoking a cigarette.

"This dude's wack," Furious said to Noah. "If he didn't pay mad cake for my beats, I wouldn't even be fucking with him."

Noah looked over his shoulder.

"No shit he's wack," Noah agreed, pushing knobs up the board.

I looked over behind the glass at the recording booth. Don Gio was groaning into a microphone and holding his hand over his headphones.

"This is making me sick," Noah said, twisting more knobs. "She's a freak."

I looked back over at the rapper whose reflective dollar sign, diamond-encrusted chain was swinging side to side. I noticed the top of a head bobbing above the soundboard. I stood on my tiptoes and saw a badly blond-highlighted woman crouched down. She appeared to be administering a blowjob. I looked up at Gio's face which crinkled and hissed like it was in agony.

I could see the woman clearer, dressed like a stripper, taking him all in. Her blue micro-mini was around her waist and she wore a bright pink bra. Her gold bangle bracelets moved as she went up and down his penis. Now, all I could hear was Don Gio's panting through the speakers.

"I'm not angry at a freak," Furious said to Noah.

I let go of the doorknob and raced down the hall as fast I could. I heard Tyran call out my name.

"Gotta skate," I said, whizzing by. "Talk to you later."

"I'll tell Noah you came by, babe," he yelled.

I ran to the elevator bank and instead opted for the quicker stairs at the side. I hailed a cab and felt disgusting the whole way home. I squirmed. Seeing cheap sex under those bright lights made me question everything. Nothing felt sacred anymore. Had it ever been?

being real & frontin'

The next morning I was back at *BeatMaker,* trying to occupy myself with menial tasks and drown myself in work. I refiled my press packets, updated my publicist phone list, and decided to transcribe my New Moon interview. Just then, Smith stopped by my desk.

"Hey, Sophie," he said. I noticed a new platinum chain hanging around his neck. It was written in Arabic.

"You're all blinged up. Get a new chain?" I asked, as he leaned on my desk.

He touched it, glancing down at his chest.

"What's it say?"

"It's Arabic script—says, 'Allah-who-akbar.' God is Great."

I nodded. Jenna had told me Smith had some 5% Nation leanings, but had also at one time, been a Farrakhan supporter in the Nation of Islam. Hey, at least he believed in something.

"Cool," I said. "So, what brings you to my desk?" I asked, looking him up.

"I wanted to say sorry about that Furious thing."

Just hearing the name Furious made my eyes well up. I was also touched by the unusual sight of Smith actually admitting a mistake. My emotions were so sore, abundant, available.

"It's okay," I croaked.

Smith leaned toward me.

"Hey. You aight?"

I held in my breath and refused to blink my eyes.

"Things didn't work out with him?" Smith asked.

I shrugged.

"You're a sweet girl, Sophie." He put his hand on my shoulder. "He's a rapper. Don't try to play a man's game. I told you industry dudes are strictly 'hit it and quit it.'"

I nodded.

"I know," I said.

"You'll be okay."

He reached for a tissue on my neighbor's desk and handed it to me. I dabbed my eyes.

"Did he get violent with you? You need us to rough him up or something? I got some friends uptown."

My mouth was agape.

"No, no." I swallowed. "I can handle it. Thanks."

"Well, if you change your mind." He punched his hands together. "I got your back."

"Thanks," I said, astonished that I could now get someone to beat someone else up, if I wanted. It was actually really sweet of Smith to offer, in a sort of twisted way.

He took off and I went back to my work.

After carefully listening to the taped banter between New Moon and me, I figured this upcoming rapper had sensed pretty early on, from my cheeky one-liners, that I liked a challenge and rarely refused a debate. I didn't start out soft and that was what had probably saved me along the way. Or got me into trouble, depending on the day.

In seventh grade, my first and favorite rap group was Public Enemy, who my brother and I discovered in our TV room (where our only AC was), Summer '89, during a powerful opening scene to Spike Lee's forthright *Do the Right Thing*. Hearing that sonic wail and Chuck D's gritty, confrontational delivery was the most exciting, badass experience of my newly minted adolescence.

In one season, I traded in my Units mall outfit for a faded black T-shirt with big block writing and a silhouette of a soldier pointing a gun through a huge target. My Mom seemed worried but went along with it, letting me play my *It Takes a Nation of Millions to Hold Us Back* tape in car rides. Maybe she reasoned that my Madonna *Like a Virgin* phase had been just as scandalous. Smart lady.

If you saw me on the street now, you might just take me for another trendy Triple Five Soul underground head or on certain Enyce days, dismiss me as a lukewarm Hot 97 listener. But—dead ass—when work boiled down and reppin' hip-hop was concerned, what greatly mattered to me was the respect of one man I'd never met: Chuck D, who Fred said, read *BeatMaker* on the regular.

So I decided to try to be more politically minded and conscious of the stories within my grasp. In that way, I'd never left that TV room with my little brother in it or the thought that somewhere out there, an intelligent emcee from Strong Island might be watching and I better act right.

That night, I was assigned to cover the annual Black Winter event in Harlem. After a succession of mainstream shows and concerts with names like "Flossin' & Blingin'" and "Platinum & Ice," I was really looking forward to a rap show centered around a worthy political mission—in this case, the freedom of former Black Panther Assata Shakur and the banning of U.S. military testing on the tiny island of Vieques, Puerto Rico. Plus, the show would keep me out of my apartment where I was alone with my self-pity.

One spring break, my part Cubana friend from college, Reina, Lucy, and I had actually vacationed on Vieques, the thankfully underdeveloped, remote island nestled in the Caribbean. It was the most beautifully pure, picturesque place I'd ever seen; and, I returned to it often in memory.

During our vacation, we spent three long, sunny days lying on the serene, secluded beach, walking along the gravel roads with roosters, stray dogs and the occasional mule crossing our path.

I listened to the Red Hot Chili Peppers' *Californication* and Remy Zero's *Villa Elaine* in my headphones at night and wrote in my journal about falling madly in love someday with an amazing guy. A guy who made me feel the way Jack did. I swear, even though we hadn't met yet, his presence was everywhere that trip—tangled in my hairbrush, dripping from my bikini, in the fine, pale sand stuck underneath my nails. Everywhere, it felt, except actually there.

Unrealized, immaterialized, a fiction.

At the last minute before the Black Winter show, I got a call from the independent publicist saying the venue was being changed because one group on the bill, dead prez, had recently been blacklisted from the spot and others around the city because authorities feared their fanship. dead prez wanted to spark a Revolution, the NYPD, it seemed, did not.

Because of pressure from the local police, the promoters were moving the show from an uptown venue by Columbia University in Harlem, to a much smaller downtown spot on St. Mark's Place where it seemed the authorities felt kids would be less likely to cause "problems."

Ethan, the photographer, had just moved to New York from Los Angeles and he was my road dawg for the night. At six, we hailed a cab from 23rd street, and tried to stuff his tripod into the trunk while the rush-hour cars behind us honked mercilessly. We hopped in and I flashed them all the finger.

"This show should be pretty cool, don't you think?"

"Yeah," I said rereading the e-mailed press release, "pretty cool."

"I'm a big dp fan. You listen to them?"

"A bit," I said holding the crumpled sheet of paper. "I'm sorry I gotta finish reading this before we get there. But I am listening to you. Multitasking."

"Cool," he said.

I wanted to make sure that I was up on the history of the event, its participants, their new releases and tours. On the bill was Common, Black Thought from The Roots, Jeru Tha Damaja, and Black Star. Stellar cast. I skimmed the artists' bios, but couldn't concentrate on the minor details. I was too distracted, too nervous, too excited.

When we pulled up to the spot on St. Mark's, there were hundreds of racially diverse backpackers (underground music fans named for wearing backpacks around) shivering in the cold and huddling in clusters. Some were gabbing on cells, or clutching tickets, trading mixtapes. I thought, *There's no way they can fit all these kids into this tiny place.* I worried the promoters would try to stuff them all in anyway.

Ethan and I jumped out of the car and pushed through some bodies to reach my homegirl Susanna, a publicist, waiting at the front door with a clipboard and an earpiece.

"Yo, this is cah-razy," I said kissing her cheek.

Her forehead was sweating.

"Girl, I know. But you guys are straight, so go ahead on in."

I looked back at Ethan and nodded.

"BeatMaker," she yelled down the hall, pointing to us.

We stopped at the press table and the afro dude behind the desk checked off my name.

"He's with you?"

"Yeah, our photographer."

"Aight," he said plucking two lanyards from the pile.

"Press room is right back there. Enjoy the show."

"One," I said as we made our way backstage.

"One," he said, returning the hip-hop farewell phrase.

Ethan and I grabbed a couple of lukewarm Coronas from the refreshment table and stood in a corner. It was mad hot, and there were only a few other reporters in the room—some with video cameras, some with just a notepad.

Only one reporter mattered to me though, my new nemesis from a competing rap magazine. He had spiky, sharp facial features, weighed like a buck twenty and stood all of five foot tall, so I knew I could take him, but he was a pushy little bastard. Napoleonic. Just then, Common came in and gave a pound to a man standing across the room. He was wearing a big green, knitted cap and flowy batik top.

My nemesis moved in and I studied his approach. He went right up and tapped Common on the back. The rapper bluntly shrugged him off and, defeated, my nemesis walked away with his head down. I decided to play it on the down low, until the Chitown emcee was done talking to his man and then, when he started back toward the stage entrance I'd move swiftly to block the door. I fixed my hair and wiped my teeth discreetly. Smile, I reminded myself. Use your feminine wiles.

"Excuse me," I said, tilting my head slightly. "We're from *Beat-Maker,* can I ask you a quick question?" Ethan was behind me, his camera ready. Over his shoulder, I noticed my nemesis was careening toward us, holding out his microphone as a weapon, his hungry eyes approaching. I needed to act fast but there was one problem:

I looked back at Common, and his gorgeousness seemed to make everything stand still—his beauty up close was awe-inspiring, striking—tall in height, broad shoulders, smooth skin, brown freckles, big clear yellow-green eyes.

"Sorry, I'm not talking to reporters tonight."

Due to his attractiveness, I had a delayed reaction to this information. I pouted.

"Well, if you get time for *one* question, it'd be great of you," I said.

He passed to the stage. I heard the bass quicken and the crowd grow louder. My nemesis made a U-turn back to his corner. *Be gone,* I said under my breath.

"We'll get him," I winked at Ethan.

He nodded skeptically.

"Since when are Californians so cynical?" I asked.

He laughed.

"I believe you," he said.

We went to watch Common's performance from the audience. The venue, which looked like a high school gym, was pretty packed and I could still see kids outside waiting. I hoped there wouldn't be a massive stampede.

"Man, this place must be at capacity," I screamed in Ethan's ear, shaking my head. And right after I said that, I looked up and saw the one hip-hop fan I prayed wouldn't be there: Jack. Standing about three feet away from me, rubbing his chin, and chatting up a skinny brunette.

I didn't really know what to do, so I just swung around to Ethan, accidentally punching him in his side with my fist. He doubled over.

"Oh my God! I'm so sorry," I said with my hand on his back, the other hand cupping my mouth. He waved me off. "No, really, I'm so sorry," I said again.

"I know," he said, rubbing his torso. "I'll be fine." I don't think he wanted me near him.

I glanced over my shoulder and there was Jack staring at me with a muddled expression. I turned my cheek again and my head was pounding. I cracked my neck and felt a heavy hand on my shoulder.

"Hey," Jack said.

I whipped around and smiled.

"Hey, look who's here!"

"Why'd you turn away when you saw me?"

"I didn't," I lied. "This is Ethan."

Jack looked him up.

"Whaddup, man?"

They smacked hands. There was a long pause. To clear things up and break the awkwardness, I said, "He's our photographer."

Jack nodded his head slowly.

"Who are you with?" I was not being inconspicuous.

"One of my roommates."

I was staring at his eyes, transfixed. He looked at me sternly.

"What is it?" I asked tilting my head. Ethan went for water and first aid.

"I'm happy to see you, that's all," he said, looking down at his feet.

Yeah right, that's all, I thought.

"It's uh. It's weird. Been a while," I said shooing hair out of my face.

The next emcee took the stage and the crowd faced front when his deejay's familiar scratch chorus began.

"I thought I might bump into you here," Jack said.

I smiled and confessed, "Working." I touched the lanyard around my neck that read PRESS.

There was so much I wanted to really tell him, ask him, but instead we just talked about the rapper onstage and how old he was looking. I guess I didn't know what was off limits with Jack or if I felt mad at him or what. Everything was so tentative with us, like we couldn't break through the top layer of our feelings and intentions.

We paused our small talk, and I just watched Jack stare at the stage. I tried to imagine how things made sense to him and if I lived in any room inside his head. It was hard to tell. At this point, did it even matter?

Ethan returned and whispered in my ear. I nodded and looked to Jack.

"I gotta go backstage for a bit."

He took a step back and slid a hand in his pocket.

"You wanna come with us?"

He smiled, said, "Yeah," and touched my open hand. It felt like he'd just switched my whole body on. That was typical Jack: just lighting me up to blow me out, like a bunch of birthday candles.

Backstage, we sat in a corner and looked around the room. He seemed a bit nervous about the scene, but watching him visibly vulnerable and starstruck was adorable. We talked about work and he told me he'd just gotten a new gig with a fashion designer.

"I'm working on her graphic design concept for fall."

"I'm sure you're working on her . . ." I cleared my throat, *"concept."*

He smiled and told me he was still dating the Cali girl, who'd moved back to LA for a while to take care of her sick grandmother. He was still mourning their distance, still feeling entitled to date other girls. *Still*—in the words of my favorite Bob Seger song—*the same.*

"Isn't the more common term 'cheating'?" I asked. He ignored me. I shook my head but didn't force the subject. I didn't want to cause more conflict or fight with him or hear raw details. I didn't want to show him it hurt. But please, what the hell kind of girl took his crap full-time? Someone needed to prescribe her some Hole and Bikini Kill quickly. Some music to give her a spine. But who was I to talk? It was "transference," according to one of Lucy's self-help books.

I immediately felt guilty for thinking that about Jenny. I'm sure Jack hadn't been straight with her either and my rash judgment was wrong and probably borne of plain old jealousy. Or maybe she was pursuing other men, too.

"Me and Jenny have an open relationship."

"Best of both worlds, eh?" I asked.

"Nah, not really," he said softly. "I miss you."

I pursed my mouth and squinted my eyes.

"Then why haven't you called me?"

"I have. And hung up on your machine. You're not the easiest person to call, Sophie."

I wondered why.

"But really, it was too hard after the last time we said good-bye," he said.

"So you stood me up at bOb bar?"

"Are you still mad about that? I was trying to warn you and I chickened out on seeing you."

I wanted to believe he was just bullshitting me, but the thing was, I couldn't. As our legs were touching in the corner of the room and my heart was beating so strong I could actually feel the warmth emanating from his body, the depressing realization of our not-togetherness was moving to the forefront.

I didn't know why we couldn't give in to anything, or why he was still with the other girl, or why we never got a fair chance.

I thought, *Damn, Jack, it's like you dissect these tiny moments, but your head's so far up the microscope (or ass), you never glimpse the big picture.*

And I couldn't keep waiting around to show him.

Unfortunately, I couldn't get myself to say any of these things out loud or ask him if I was right, even though I wanted to so desperately. It just seemed too tense, and I felt too manipulated. Instead, I chumped out and called it a day with, "Well, I should probably find Ethan and get back to work."

He nodded slowly. We both stood up and looked at each other. He held my wrist.

"Are you still with that rapper? 'Cause Noah tells me he's been up at Landmark with some other females, if you know what I mean."

I looked away. He needed to hear it from me.

"I want you, Jack. But I can't have you. So instead, like a dumb ass, I slept with Furious. You should just know because I'm sure it's going around anyway."

Jack gasped.

"You slept with him?"

There was a warped, almost powerful pleasure in hurting Jack at this moment.

"He was my friend at one point," I said. "It was a mistake and I'm gonna confront him about it."

"God, Sophie, I'm so sorry about dragging you into everything with Jenny."

"You don't have to feel sorry for me, and you're not to blame for everything."

He pawed his chest and looked way up at the roof, rafters, sky. I was taken aback by his candidness.

"I understand it's hard," I said, swallowing a big lump in my throat.

He looked down at his feet.

"I don't want to lose you forever. I know I'll regret it," he said. He reached out and tucked some of my hair behind my ears.

I was exasperated with us too. I put my hand on his shoulder. "Call me if your situation changes," I said and sighed. "I haven't given up on you yet," I whispered. It seemed like the only solution was to wait.

As I walked away, I wondered if he'd ever realize he was repeating a mistake by letting me leave each time or if he knew he was taking risks and just did it anyway. One part of me hoped he'd suffer losing me, but the other part wanted him to be happy and that made me hate him even more.

The verdict seemed to have been passed down in the case of Jack vs. Sophie. Now, he would never really get to know me: that I'd once fainted in a Foo Fighters mosh pit and woke up alone on the side stage terrified. That in one small moment, I think I really loved him. He might have liked to know that he'd been my Bonita, existed as my Grace, and suffered as my Blue Valentine. Maybe, but for myriad reasons, that conversation had not been born.

big pimpin'

A couple of days later, I was due at the swanky W Hotel in tourist-infested Times Square with a different score to settle with a guy. The main lobby elevator was by a chic, neon-decorated bar that seductively whispered my name, followed by the evil words "tequila shot." I ignored its demonic call and instead, took the lift up to twenty-three, minding my own biz. Immediately on the floor, a couple of tall, bejeweled black men passed me by. I recognized their pungent, yet pleasant scent as Platinum Chanel.

I got to the room and knocked on the door. No answer. I glanced at my watch: 6:54 p.m., six minutes early. I tried again harder this time. The door flung open and a white, skinny, ponytail-and-Marc-Jacobs-wearing woman greeted me. She had a hands-free phone cord in her ear and a two-way in her hand, the publicist uniform. With bug eyes and a cold fish grip, she informed me they were running behind. Big surprise! I asked how long. She said almost an hour. I nodded and she invited me inside to wait.

There was Nelly on the edge of a bed, dressed all in white-and-red Vokal, a bright camera light illuminating his face and a young black guy holding a microphone and notebook. The camera guy said he was ready. The publicist and I leaned against the wall, looking on. As I listened in, the journalist's questions seemed more comprehensive than the ones I'd planned on asking, so I stole his inquiry about Nelly playing baseball.

At the end of their interview, the reporter asked Nelly to do a couple of drops for their cable-access TV show, and the rapper politely complied.

Then, another white dude from an entertainment Web site went. He asked mostly the same questions. It occurred to me that when these artists 'do Press,' they spend the whole day reciting the same facts over and over again: how they got the particular name for the album, if he was dating Eve (coy denial), did he expect the same success as his astonishing debut units? The monotony was incredible, even just standing there and observing for an hour.

Next was my turn, but as I approached Nelly and smiled, he blurted out,

"When can I eat?"

This famished scenario was creepily familiar.

The publicist said they were getting him pizza.

"I can wait until it comes," I said, leaning on a wall.

"No, we have to make up time," the publicist chided.

I shrugged and just then the pizzas marched through the door on the arms of weary assistants.

Between the wires, press packs, cameras, and clothes, the young ladies couldn't find a proper place to set down the large boxes so they dropped them on the floor. Nelly crouched down to the boxes and since no one had gotten plates, he'd held the flimsy, cheesy triangle in his hand while trying to take a bite. This was not a multi-platinum rapper's most glamorous moment, I must say.

"C'mon," he said pointing to the bed. For a moment, I pictured us as lovers: me removing the Band-Aid from his handsome cheek and kissing his juicy lips. But then he asked,

"What's your name?" and the fantasy burst.

"Sophie." I eyed the pizza slice he now folded. He took a bite. My stomach grumbled.

"What up, Sophie?"

"Hey. Are you sure you don't want to wait so you can chew your food in like, peace?"

He smiled.

"It's all good. I can eat and talk at the same time," he said.

So that's just what we did.

"Why didn't you become a baseball player?" I asked.

(This was the question I shamelessly lifted from the last reporter.)

"There are a lot of things you use in sports that you can apply to the rap game."

"Like what?"

"When you're up to bat, you gotta make a big play. That's how I feel about my rap team too. I came up to plate first and I gotta get us to the World Series."

"I think you're already there," I said, remembering his mind-boggling multimillion-dollar album sales.

He grinned. There was a piece of tomato stuck in between his gold front teeth.

He was polite and sweet and soft-spoken and excitable, the kind of guy that gives you all of his attention—as though you're the only girl in the world—until another girl comes into the room and he forgets you're around. In between the mozzarella and pepperoni, I thought we'd made a friendly connection anyway. (Crush #37 on a rapper I'd interviewed.) When I filed the story for *BeatMaker,* Fred was extra pleased that I'd asked him about baseball.

Not long after the Nelly interview, I was at a different midtown hotel for a lunch meeting and I noticed Nelly's publicist and the same guys from the hallway all sitting around in the lobby. I went over and said hey. Then Nelly came down with Eve on his arm, looking very couple-like and beaming in a morning-after glow. She was slim, dressed all in pink, and her permed hair was highlighted blond—a far cry from her earlier incarnation as a tough, thick, Philly Ruff Ryder.

I bit my pen. So it was true.

His publicist immediately looked up at me and pleaded for me not to report on what I'd just seen.

"I have to," I replied. "It's too juicy," I explained.

She laughed. "Damn, why'd you have to see that?"

"They looked like they were in a good mood."

She put her head in her hands.

"Hey, I'll be discreet," I said. "I won't mention the hotel or anything."

I looked over at Nelly, who'd been stopped by some ten-year-old–looking boys and their yuppie dad. He was signing autographs as the three gazed at him in awe, like he was a statue or something. Eve went unrecognized.

When I got back to the office, I put the story on *BeatMaker*'s Web site. HP, my editor on the gossip piece, pressured me to include the exact location saying, "You work for us, not Nelly." I argued that wasn't fair to do.

"He's still staying there," I said. "If I say what hotel he's at, he'll get mobbed."

HP eventually conceded. High-profile gossip columns and media outlets immediately picked up the tasty item.

I was working from home and heard Eve on the radio being interviewed by Ed and Dre. They asked her about being seen with Nelly at the hotel. She denied the whole situation saying, "Don't believe everything you read."

This anti-journalistic sentiment pissed me right off. I was *there,* I'd been the one to see them with my own peepers and here she was lying about it! Yeah, it's true that everything in print should be taken with a grain of salt, but this morsel was credible. I was credible. Thus, I learned my own valuable lesson: Don't believe everything a rapper or any celeb says either.

trippin'

My *BeatMaker* position seemed to be paying off as Dana okayed my Nelly interview copy on the first pass and rappers were becoming the highlight of my day. Plus, I got promoted to a better desk by the window.

I trudged through the stress of late night closes, temperamental coworkers, and cookie-cutter industry parties and derived my real pleasure from interviewing artists who were making moves. Surprisingly, work seemed to be the one avenue of my life that was willing to meet me halfway. It was the best distraction I had.

The following week, I found myself headed to Landmark for an invite-only listening party to preview an upcoming Tornado album. But, before attending that, I was asked by HP to stop by SOB's and see if I could nab an OutKast interview on the fly. We had word the Atlanta duo was performing an unannounced Tribeca gig in support of their impending release, *Stankonia*. Fred had tickets to The Nuyorican Poets Café, so I was next in line. I had no choice but to come through.

"And catch a quick interview with their opening act, too. 'Five Percent.' They got a buzz," HP demanded.

The thing that rang so true about just getting your foot in the door was that by the year double-oh, rap music and culture were exploding into the mainstream. It was the year—millennium—hip-hop *became* pop culture.

So popular and lucrative was the scene and interested were the masses that *BeatMaker* was drowning in stories, interviews and content—trying to satiate fans' appetites. This chaotic time was perfect for a once peripheral, but always available and eager new journalist like me. When your higher-ups are debating choices between Jay-Z and the Neptunes, Mystikal versus Mannie Fresh, and fielding offers daily to interview Swizz Beatz and Lil' Kim, among other A-Listers, then breaking you off some OutKast story was not a big deal.

One day, I hoped to be the one actually picking the artists for review, but these days, the leftovers were pretty amazing.

I left *BeatMaker* a little early so I could make it home for a quick shower and to wash my greasy hair. (I was in a bad habit of only washing my mane about once a week to conserve blowouts.)

I turned on NPR and indulged in some talk radio. I needed a little break from blaring music and any thought in lyrical form. Instead, I enjoyed the comforting tales of *This American Life*. The taste of seeing Jack recently at the show was still on my tongue. He sure made me sad, but after him hurting my heart repeatedly, I was almost used to it. Wait, that kind of made me sadder.

I decided to wear a black flamenco-inspired lacy top with slim black slacks and black slip-ons to SOB's. Yes, I was in a full-on dark period, the New York costume. Spring had sprung, but I hadn't yet.

The camera guy, Jim, met me at the venue at 6 p.m., right by the backstage entrance. The show was popping off at exactly 7 p.m., which gave us about an hour to sneak our camera inside and set it up for some b-roll of the show. We had a hint around the office, after HP nabbed a bootleg of *Stankonia,* that it was gonna blow, so Jim and I felt extra pressure to get the story. Somehow, I would try to finagle my sneaky self backstage and hunt down Andre and Big Boi for a quick, exclusive Q&A. Oh, and Five Percent (whose catchy-as-hell single, "Buyaka," was climbing the charts.) This shaky plan felt like some covert military operation. I clutched my now trusty Mead notebook in my clammy hands—this would be my single weapon.

We got to the head of the long entrance line and mentioned we were on the press list. The bouncer eyed Jim's bag.

"I need to search that," he said pointing at the sack. Jim's face fell.

The bouncer reached inside and took out the camera. He shook his head.

"No recording inside." He popped out the cartridge and threw it into a box. Jim begged him for the film back but to no avail. Now, the pressure on me increased twofold.

"Fuck, I should have thought to put an extra tape in my socks or something," Jim said.

I patted him on the back.

"I'll try to get us a little sumthin sumthin," I reassured.

I'd never seen SOB's so crowded with people. Every corner was accounted for, every inch occupied by an eager OutKast lover.

I eyed the backstage bouncer who was a tall, plumpy, pasty Russian-looking dude in blue T-shirt pacing by the entranceway. He acted and looked coked up—jittery and sweaty. I decided I should just try and not think about it too much and just storm the door.

I approached him and said that I was expected backstage and that I was part of the press. He shook his head.

I pleaded for him to let me through, but he was immovable.

"Look, I have my notebook. I'm a member of the press, I swear. I just can't find the Arista publicist right now but I'm supposed to be back there." I caught Jim out the corner of my eye, ordering a drink at the bar. "Please." I held my notebook up higher and shook it for dramatic effect.

He was silent.

"Why would I be carrying this stupid notebook if I wasn't part of the press?"

This question seemed to trip him up. He pinched his nose and suddenly unhooked the velvet rope and let me stride through.

Holy shit!

"Thank you," I said curtly, concealing my awe. I briskly walked down the stairs before the guy came to. I marched past the VIP coat check and heard some noise behind a door. I took a deep breath and knocked hard. The door flew open and a tall man dressed like Bootsie Collins answered.

"Hey," I said as though I were some casual caller. "I'm press," I said holding up my notebook. He shrugged and let me through.

"Come on in, Press," he said with a southern drawl.

When I did, I saw the entire Dungeon Family draped over the couches. The Mardi Gras–looking group grew silent when I entered but I pretended to know where I was going and plopped myself next to a guy I recognized from the Goodie Mob. His teeth were almost all gold. The talking resumed and everyone kind of ignored my presence. Someone tapped me on the shoulder and I flinched. I looked up, there was a blunt in my face. I shook my head no and said "thanks though."

It was very obvious I was the odd person out and not just because I was the only non-black, because no one knew who the hell I was. Still, no one bothered to ask. I kept my head down and doodled in my notebook (flowers, always). I eyed the refreshments on the table across the room, wishing against odds I could crack open that two-liter of Diet Pepsi and quench my thirst. Instead, I sat there like an extra pillow and everyone just continued on as usual.

I fidgeted with my purse, took out my cell phone, put it back in my bag. Debated actually walking across the room to fetch the pop. Sighed. Finally got up the nerve to walk across to the refreshments. Added some Jack to my Pepsi to take the edge off. Went back to my spot on the couch. Chewed on my straw. Slurped my drink. All the while, flying fairly low, like an undetectable stealth missile traveling under the radar. Time moved very slowly.

The group was now talking about the upcoming Mardi Gras parade in New Orleans. I kept my head down and my eyes up, picking up buzz words like "beads" and "bras."

Soon after, Andre and Big Boi entered. I eyed them as they walked into the cramped room. They announced they had to change their clothes so they headed to a closet directly in front view of me.

They didn't bother shutting the door so I didn't bother looking away. Hell, I am human. I watched them piece together their outfits and undress, both of them mighty attractive and manly in their own saucy ways. Yum.

I was lusting when the door flung open and a dark chocolate–skinned guy dressed all in black entered with two tall bodyguards behind him. It was Puff Daddy. Mister "I invented the Remix" himself. People stood up to give him a pound as he made his way across the room. My cheeks were burning up. All I could see was the giant diamond cross swinging from side to side as he made his way closer to me. Shit, I didn't know if I should get up and greet the man or just try to blend into the couch. He didn't seem real friendly. As I debated, he stood right in front of me, scrunched his grill into a "Who the hell is she?" crooked way. I shot up and put out my hand fully meaning to introduce myself as a journalist.

"I thought you were innocent," is unfortunately what fell out of my mouth instead.

Time stood still and everyone turned their heads.

"Excuse me?" he asked, raising his eyebrows.

I gulped.

"In the club," I said, dying a slow death.

He paused to consider my idiocy.

"Okay, whatever," he said, shrugging me off and moving to the next person.

I sank back into my spot. Well, that was successful. Nice job, Sophie. I wiped my sweaty hands on my clothes.

Andre and Big Boi piled out of the closet. Andre looked like

Hansel, dressed in neon orange lederhosen and a fedora. His other half was more gangsta in a fuzzy Kangol, platinum chain and black T-shirt. They talked to Puff for a moment, then a guy headed in and said they were due onstage in a few moments. Half the Family moved out. I realized it was now or never but the two were still kicking it with Mr. Bad Boy. They broke up and the duo moved to the hallway. I ejected from the couch and trailed them.

As soon as I turned the corner, I bumped right into Andre.

"Hey," I said tapping him on the shoulder. "I'm from *Beat-Maker*. Can I ask you a quick question before you take the stage?"

"Sure," he said with a smooth grin and honeyed Georgia accent. He looked like he had all the time in the world. Realistically, I had maybe fifteen seconds to mine a quote from him that I could use in my concert review.

"You've got a real buzz with *Stankonia*. What distinguishes your music from other rap groups?"

"We just love making our original music. It's eclectic, like cricket booty."

"Cricket booty?"

"Yeah, our music sounds like cricket booty."

"I see." I jotted down the mysterious phrase in my book. "So, what are your expectations for the new album?"

"Ten million," he smiled.

"Ambitious," I nodded.

People filtered by us heading up and down the stairs. A guy came over and fiddled with Andre's mic. Big Boi reappeared. I made notes.

"OutKast, you're on!" yelled a voice from up top.

Andre looked at me.

"You got what you need, baby?"

I nodded.

"Thanks so much," I said, touching his wrist. "Have a good show."

And with those parting words, Andre and Big Boi took the stage with abandon.

I look down at my scribbles. Cricket booty? I didn't know exactly what the hell that meant, but it was just charming and quirky enough to fly back at the office. People would expect a phrase like that from OutKast.

I needed to keep moving to complete my mission. I bolted back into the green room before I got caught by the creepo doorman and worse, embarrassed myself in front of musicians I admired.

When I re-entered the room, the group Five Percent was wiping their faces with towels, chugging apple juice, and heading into the closet to change. I knew it would only be a matter of moments before someone would notice me, so I kept the pressure on and busted through the changing door.

"Damn, Gina," one of the members yelled, standing up in his BVDs. Other members were undressing down to their birthday suits.

"Hey, sorry. Just wanted to ask you all a quick question about the performance." I saw a big penis waving at me and hid my eyes with my hand.

"You think this is the Giants' locker room or something, lady?" I heard another member say.

They all started laughing. I followed.

"I'm not crazy, I swear." Then, I realized where I was. "Okay, I am a little crazy." I pinched my fingers together. "But this is for *BeatMaker*. I'm legit." I held up my trusty notebook.

Silence. We were all in shock. This was some kind of scrappy, vigilante journalism. I bet they didn't teach this in J-School.

"So what's your question, crazy girl?" a voice asked.

I took a deep breath and dropped my hand down, taking in the full, bountiful view.

"What's special about playing in New York?"

"Crazy fans like you," the BVD guy said, cracking a smile.

"The audience is tough, but once you prove you're hot, they start wylin' out," said Penisman.

I nodded, wanting to get out of there before all of the professionalism thing went awry.

"Perfect. Thanks," I said, scooting away.

When I got back into the crowd upstairs, I felt like a queen who'd survived an overthrow attempt. The exhilaration of talking to OutKast, hanging backstage, seeing Puffy, and *really* seeing Five Percent was like a giant wave I was surfing or a black diamond mountain I was boarding.

I got to Jim who said he'd been worried about me.

"Where'd you go?" he asked.

I smiled big as OutKast launched into the frenetic pulse of "B.O.B." and the crowd erupted, bouncing around like exploding popcorn.

I leaned into his ear and screamed, "Backstage!"

He took a step back, shook his head in disbelief and laughed.

Then he gave me a massive hug, squeezing me so hard he lifted my feet off the ground.

"You got the OutKast quote?" he yelled.

I nodded.

"What about Five Percent?" he asked.

I laughed.

"Oh, I got more than a quote from those guys." I smiled. I touched my temple. "It's all up here." I smiled.

I felt really proud that I'd come through—truly self-satisfied. But, I also had to conquer a bigger challenge, the listening session at Landmark. It was in that moment that I wished my personal life hadn't infected my job so much. My love life and my work needed a separation. No, make that a divorce.

The cab pulled up in front of Landmark. There were a couple of tall black guys and one Asian kid smoking bidis and cigarettes. I smoothed down my hair, hopped out the car and avoided eye contact, catching a whiff of the earthy-smelling smoke on the sidewalk.

The Landmark party was for Tornado, a gritty rap duo from Brick City who were staging a comeback with the underground heads. Maybe the studio was someplace I should've avoided, and it did kind of scare me because I'd probably come face-to-face with Furious, but I liked doing things that were terrifying. Plus, he needed to be checked for dissing me. I was gonna call him out on not calling me. I felt confident after my performance at the concert.

I took the elevator up with a couple of tall, handsome guys who looked like identical twins: one was sporting a gaudy Sean John tee and sweatpants; the other was decked out in a Mecca jean coordinate. I was wondering if there'd be any other industry woman representing tonight to feel some solidarity with. I didn't get my hopes up.

"You going to the listening session?" one of the guys asked me.

I nodded. I recognized one of them as a model for Phat Farm. They were probably both models, I figured from their buffed manicured nails shining with clear polish. They were well-groomed and rich-looking. I could smell their spicy cologne.

On the short ride up, I was already beginning to chicken out on confronting Furious. I decided that if we had an encounter, I'd just say hey and keep it moving. One thing you can usually count on with men is that they're happy to avoid confrontation.

As soon as the Landmark elevator doors opened, my stomach hit the floor. The smell of weed, the familiar black light, the same bulletproof window, all brought back a million mental pictures. I commanded my body to move. I led the way to the window with Sean John and Mecca in tow. I steadied my hand on the wood frame and knocked on the glass. I saw the Rawkus T-shirt first, but it was his thick wrists that gave him away. The hot dude. He leaned toward me and grabbed the window.

"Yo," he said, looking at me and then at the guys over my shoulder.

"Sophie Drakas," I smiled, pointing for the guys to go next.

"Carl and Palmer Thompson."

The guy grabbed a clipboard and crossed our names off the press list.

"I'm gonna buzz you in," he said.

I headed for the bathroom first and splashed some cold water on my neck. I'd look for Tyran and Noah when I got out. I needed backup to get me through this evening. Was it brave or stupid of me to go out alone all the time?

When I got up, I stood against a wall in the hallway under a red light and observed the madness of this event. Rappers had signed the wall and I leaned next to Kurtis Blow's large autograph tagged in bubble letters.

I noticed that (not surprisingly) the event was more a "party" than a "listening session." There was a fuzzy speaker above my head but all I could hear was a faint duntduntdunt coming out. Hardly anyone was paying attention to the music, but because it was my job, I at least tried. Of course there were like ten guys to every female to distract me, to dissect.

The four white guys I counted all had Caesar haircuts, except for curly-haired Kevin, who whooshed by me in a green button-up and khaki pants. Some people passed mixtapes. A group of black guys were spitting rhymes in the corner, slapping hands and egging one another on. I noticed a lot of people coming out the backroom with plates of food, so I made a mental note to get back there ASAP. Except I was too intimated and scared to leave my wall.

Most of the folks around me were chatting on the cells or text-messaging on two-ways. A couple were actually scribbling into notebooks. Some publicist thought by blaring the music he'd get folks into it, but all that did was make everyone scream. I finally moved into the family room where a temporary bar had been put up. The bartender looked totally spent and his tip jar was empty. He was slammed with people. I pushed through the mass to get a pop.

"Four Thug Passions," a guy over my shoulder yelled out, holding up his fingers.

Nothing like an open bar!

Two guys in front of me were arguing and debating. All I heard was,

"There's a definite connection between that politico and M.O.P.'s 'How About Some Hardcore.' Don't you agree?"

I rolled my eyes and figured they were from *Rolling Stone* or something.

I got to the front of the mass and eyed the free booze—Hennessey, Alizé, Courvoisier, Heineken—the usual suspects. I tossed the pop idea and went for a beer. Onto food next. I made my way through a mushroom cloud of THC and entered the backroom.

The spread—green beans, corn bread, fried chicken, catfish, mac-n-cheese—gave me the impression that the record label really wanted to floss and had hooked up the catering from a soul food spot uptown like Amy Ruth's, or Soul Fixin's on Eighth Avenue in midtown, or even Justin's on the West Side.

My mouth watered as I piled my plate with gooey mac-n-cheese and cornbread. To my stomach this meant a nice meal; to my ears this meant this album must be really crappy. There's a simple ratio for a listening session: the better the food and alcohol is, the worse the album is.

I took a seat on the edge of the couch, next to a beautiful, curvaceous woman who resembled Tyra Banks and smelled like strawberries. The studio was packed with faces, moving in slow-mo, in and out of the rooms.

Across the way, I noticed one of my favorite emcees chatting up two girls with mini-backpacks and stringy blond hair. He was middle-aged now, but still attractive. Folks gossiped about his Ecstasy habit and constant philandering, especially with any Anglo ladies who'd have him.

I sighed and continued scanning the scene while drinking my beer; it seemed every guy was either palming a cognac glass or smoking a cigar or telecommunicating.

Eventually, Noah and Tyran appeared at the end of the couch, screaming my name like rowdy troublemakers.

"There she is!" Tyran said, pointing at me.

I shook my head and, jokingly, hid my face.

"Soooooophie," Noah said as though he were announcing me onstage. "We can still see you." He tickled me.

I stood up to greet them. They were extra-friendly.

"Where'd you run to the other night, girl?" Tyran asked.

"I forgot I had to be home for a call." I stumbled. "Are you guys bent or what?" I said, deflecting the topic to their inebriated state.

"I hope so," Noah said.

"Otherwise, there's really no excuse for our behavior," Tyran added.

"True," I smiled.

While Noah went to fetch more beers, Tyran casually mentioned that Noah and his girlfriend had recently hit splitsville.

"That's too bad," I said. I didn't want Tyran to think I was interested in pursuing something with Noah. I knew beyond a doubt that I was currently maxed out with men. And my heart and hopes were still with both of them.

"He'll bounce back, fa shizzle," Tyran said.

I nodded.

"Yes, Snoop," I smiled.

Noah returned and sat down next to me, and I noticed his calloused hands as he folded them in his lap.

"So, sup ma?"

"Well, ya know, just tryna eat," I said in a mock-gangsta voice.

He fell out laughing.

"And you?" I asked bumping his shoulder.

"Just working mostly. Grindin' and hangin' out a bit. I'm going to Miami in a couple of weeks for a vacation."

We sipped our green bottles and stared at the wall.

"You talked to Jack lately?"

I huffed.

"I doubt Jack even remembers me these days."

"Yeah, right," Noah challenged.

I bit my lip and looked away. The party was popping off now—folks passing blunts and bidis, playing pool, cards and skeelo in the corner, bobbing their heads to the music. "You still hangin' out with Furious?" he asked.

I shrugged.

"I wouldn't say that exactly . . ."

"Okay, okay."

"Is he here?"

"I haven't seen him yet, but he's supposed to stop by."

"Yeah, we need to talk."

Noah touched my hand.

"You should call Jack. He's got news," he said.

I paused. His hand was still on mine, but not in a romantic way just in a very kind way. I put my head on his shoulder.

"Thanks, Noah, for being my friend."

He nodded.

"No problem."

The bond me, Tyran, Noah, and even Furious shared was hip-hop. The industry. And Landmark. We knew much of the rap scene was processed garbage, but at its core, the music still counted. No matter how much of the industry was pretense, the real shit was still so real and powerful and moving that it was still more relevant and sincere than a lot of "art" in this world and in our generation.

"You wanna go back to the office and burn a branch?" Tyran asked.

"Sure, but I don't smoke," I said. Marijuana (aka trees, weed, broccoli), you might have noticed, was practically a job requirement in the biz.

"Come on," Noah said, helping me up.

I followed the guys down the narrow hallway and looked around for Furious. Head down, eyes up. I couldn't tell if it was because I did or didn't want to see him. It's called the first-guy-you-slept-with syndrome. He was my Berlin wall, halving my heart between love and hate.

"Kevin's got a rough of the new Kool G Rap album on his desk that we can swipe," Tyran said as he went to open the door to the backroom offices. Me and Noah stood at the doorway waiting to enter.

The door flung open and there was Furious, pants down and in mid-thrust with the Tyra Banks look-alike, who was splayed out on a desk in a beyond comprising position. All I heard were voices out of breath and squishy noises.

"Eww," was all I could say.

Furious turned to us bug-eyed, pulled out of her, and quickly buttoned up his pants. Within seconds, the woman had dressed herself and waltzed right past us like nothing had happened.

We stood in the same place—Tyran still had his hand on the knob and Noah hadn't budged from my side. I couldn't feel anything.

"That is not cool, dude," Tyran shook his head at Furious. "That's my desk."

"Sorry, man," Furious returned, looking at both the guys, averting his gaze from my direction.

"It's digusting," Noah said.

"If you guys don't mind giving us a second. I want to talk to Earnest alone," I said to them.

"Earnest?" Tyran asked.

"You sure you'll be okay?" Noah asked.

I nodded, walked inside the offices and shut the door behind me.

"You owe me an explanation," I said, noticing his buckle was still undone.

He stepped back away from me and sat in a chair. He lit a Newport. I stayed standing, folded my arms and waited.

"So?"

"What do you want from me? I fucked up."

"I agree." I wanted to slap the smug right out of him. I was seething inside, but I told myself to be rational. I'd been waiting for this moment for too long to blow it by just screaming my head off. "Lemme ask you something."

"You can ask me anything, Sophie," he said, exhaling.

"Give me one of those," I said.

He reached the pack out to me and I chose one.

"Were we ever friends?"

"What do you think?" he asked.

"I asked first," I said, taking a drag.

"Yeah, we were. But I freaked out after we slept together when you said . . . well, you know . . ."

"I know," I said, looking down at my feet.

"I could've handled it better, been a man about it. But listen, I'm taking the L for my part. The blame."

"Why didn't you return my phone call? *Calls.*"

"Because," he said, stubbing out his menthol. "I didn't know what to say and I knew you'd freak out."

I shook my head.

"Don't talk smack about me. All I did was be naive."

"Look, can't we just move past this and be friends or what?"

"Are you kidding?" I asked. "What kind of a friend ignores you like that?"

"See, that's what I mean. Everything is such a big deal to you."

He stood up. I looked him dead in the eyes. I thought about burning him with my cigarette and how satisfactory it'd be to injure him, but then I thought I'd already expended way too much energy on this guy. He was a loser. A scared little boy who I let break my heart.

"Fuck it. It's over," I said, reaching for the ashtray. "I'm done." I left him standing there and went for the door. The front door. All the way out to the street where I hailed a cab home. In the ride crosstown, I decided every moment from that point on was a chance for change. A reconciliation. At least Furious had given me that: a closed door and a fresh start and some lessons learned.

Just like a Loretta Lynn song, I was not going to let this pathetic guy pull everything, even my dignity, from underneath me. I had been wronged and I knew it. But there was no point pushing the thing. It died and as Beck sings, *We live again.*

When I got home, I made two phone calls: one to Lucy, where I left a fragmented message on her answering machine telling her it was urgent and to call me back; the second call went out to Happy Noodles for some delivery veggie dumpling soup to assuage my churning alcohol-and-anxiety stomach.

I was already slurping through my broth and watching QVC when the phone rang back. My body jolted. It was Lucy. I gave her the deal about the confrontation with Furious.

"I'd dreamed about getting to ask him all these questions, but I forgot most of them in the moment and his answers were so hollow and nothing and inconclusive. So, I just gave up. Anyway, who has a good deflowering story, right? They all suck," I said. I had a flash-black of him and the girl on the desk. I gripped the phone tighter.

"Drama," she concluded. "You can't help it, you're a writer so you're drawn to that but remember, you don't have to live your life like Courtney Love or Lauryn Hill to have it matter. Seriously. It's not about that."

I started crying and wiped some tears with my soy-stained napkin.

"I'm not trying to be hard on you, Sophie, but most of these hip-hop guys with this hyper macho thing, let 'em go. They're a waste of your time. Leave the aggravation to your real work, your job, which I'll remind you now, you're pretty amazing at."

Every blunt word poked at my skin, but it made sense and what I needed now more than ever was some understanding of my motivations—work, love, me. We hung up.

Further "understanding" would come later, so in the meantime I'd self-medicate. I took some Tylenol PM out of the medicine cabinet and put on Dolly Parton's *White Limozeen*. I lay in bed and her innocent, childlike voice carried me to another place. It made me feel calm. I passed out in my clothes and makeup.

I called in sick the next day (but still had to squeeze in this preplanned Ludacris phoner from home) and the few days after that, faking food poisoning (which I knew nobody believed, but still didn't challenge). I watched MTV2 until I was dizzy, ignored the phone and Hotmail, took shower after shower, knit furiously, bit my nails, knotted my hair, wanted my mom.

Every music video reminded me of a boy I'd dated—so much so, that I thought they should just start a whole channel devoted to my romantic failures and get it all over with. I dove so low that at one point, I even considered purchasing on Amazon an Alanis Morissette or Ani DiFranco CD.

For those three days, home was like a trap where I kept bumping into myself. I dreaded going to sleep, having to turn out the lights and lay in the dark with my feelings and fears.

The only thing that helped me was playing my favorite tape from the seventh grade, New Edition's *Heart Break*. Seriously. I guess I just needed to hear something innocuous and bland that reminded me of home and innocence and being a young girl full of fairy-tale dreams of love.

In the middle of the night, after rewinding "Can You Stand the Rain" about ten times, I'd imagine that everything would all turn out okay. That Jack was holding me. That feeling this deserted was temporary. That I'd heal from this whole mess and gain control again. That something would come along to give me my spirit back. Maybe I'd come back to rescue myself.

I called my brother and woke him again. He confirmed my deep malaise.

"Give it time, Sophie. It's a big thing and you just got knocked down a bit," he said over the phone. I was sitting on my bed in the pitch-black.

I was ready to put a cap on the exile from the job and outside for fear of diving any deeper. I mean, hello, I was listening to New Edition on repeat—regressing to my awkward pubescence. What kind of masochist wants to feel like she's thirteen again?

I got up from bed, washed my face, and made some warm milk with a lump of sugar. I sat on the couch and hugged my blanket. I was watching reruns of *Good Times* when my phone rang. I looked at the VCR time blinking midnight and yawned. I debated even answering it.

"Hello?" I asked, afraid of who might be on the other end.

"Okay, I know it's late . . ."

Lucy? I could hardly make out her voice over the loud background noise of people jabbering, blaring drum-n-bass, and police sirens.

"Are you at a concert?" I asked.

"No, babe, I'm in your neighborhood. My coworkers just left me. Come out!" she screamed.

I looked down at my pjs and played with a bobby pin in my hair. The offer to go drinking didn't seem tempting; except, I would be getting out of the apartment.

"I'm sleeping!" I screamed back.

"Unlikely," she snapped. "Get your ass to the Swine On Nine right now. You owe me a Cosmo."

"Ninth Avenue?" I asked.

"Uh-huh." I could hear another female patron asking for the pay phone. (Lucy was the last person in NYC who didn't own a cell.)

"Fine," I surrendered. "Give me a half hour."

"A half hour?" she whined.

I hung up, scooted in my slippers to my closet and put on a pair of jeans and a comfy wool sweater. The place was a dive and I didn't care what I looked like anyway. After dressing, I had just enough energy to brush out my hair.

I made my way to the bar. Twelve-thirty a.m. on Wednesday in any other place I could think of would be lifeless, but in Manhattan where the bars don't close until 4 a.m., the party's just getting crunk.

And when I arrived at the bar, I realized my friend Lucy was leading the debauchery.

"I don't think I've ever seen you this wasted," I said.

She clutched the bar with one hand and smoked a Parliament with the other like freaking Mae West or something. She ignored me and shrugged.

"I had a bad day at work. Sue me," she said, spraying fine droplets of saliva in my direction. Any screen siren classiness evaporated. "I'm so happy you came out. I love you. Let's go to Black Star Bar. I'll pay for the cab."

"But I just got here," I said, eyeing a free stool.

"That guy Noah is deejaying," she said.

"How do you know?"

She socked my arm and started laughing.

"You told me the other day, retard."

Yes, now I remembered.

"Fine, I'll go. But just one drink." She was a convincing actress and I was too weak to argue.

So that's just what we did.

It was packed inside the lounge—all Kangol caps, girls in strappy sandals, haze, and loud music. We blew past the bar and pool table and right into the back room. Lucy and I ordered drinks from a waitress. We drank them in the corner. I really just wanted my bed. Some male stranger stopped by, rolled a blunt, and asked me and Lucy if we wanted some.

"This is some Uptown shit. It'll trip you out, so be careful."

I couldn't tell if he thought that was good or bad.

"No," I said. "I don't smoke."

"No, thanks," Lucy said. "I'm sticking to booze."

"You sure?" he asked.

I noticed a guy in a Yankees cap whose slouch reminded me of Jack. I missed him so much. I wanted to self-destruct.

"Fine," I said. "Hand it over." I took a long drag. Another. And another.

"Easy," he said. "It's take two and pass." He snatched it back from me.

My eyelids started to feel like cinder blocks. I was standing, but my body felt like it was riding a roller coaster. I took another hit.

The guy smoked a bit more and stubbed the cigar out in the ashtray on the bar. Lucy's head expanded like an inflatable balloon and she disappeared.

"*Fly* lot high set," the guy whispered in my ear and walked away. It sounded like he was speaking in code. I couldn't find Lucy so I walked outside and got in a cab. Everything was fast-paced. Pumped up. Whooshing by.

He stopped at an intersection, I opened the door and vomited on the curb.

Next thing I knew, I was walking into some bright, white light. A woman met me and took my hand.

"Mom?" I asked.

She shook her head.

"It feels like my heart is going to come out," I said, slurring my words. "Is it?" I asked.

She took me to a hard bed and I fell dead asleep.

"What did you take?" A male voice asked over and over again, stirring my brain into motion.

My eyes felt glued shut. I forced them open. I had a tube in my arm. I was too knocked out to freak.

"Sophie, what did you take?"

I looked up at the man in blue.

"I smoked something," I grumbled. My mouth felt like a desert.

"Marijuana?" he asked, not letting up.

I ached to remember. My body was sore and my head was torturing me with pain. I nodded carefully.

"Was there any PCP in it?" he asked loudly.

"I don't know. Where am I?" I managed to ask.

"St. Vincent's Hospital. A cab dropped you off last night. Do you remember that?"

"Yes, sir," I said. It was coming back a bit, in parts. "Can I have some water? I'm so thirsty."

A nurse brought me a Dixie Cup. I tried to drink the liquid, but my mouth refused to swallow it. The doctor got a page and had to leave. The nurse walked over to my bedside.

"Your friend Lucy is in the lobby waiting to take you home. You were really dehydrated last night and having some hallucinations, okay?"

"That's not okay," I said, trying again to swallow.

She smiled.

"No, it's not. I take it back."

My eyes stung. I'd scared the shit out of myself. She softly patted my forehead with a cool cloth.

"Thank you," I said, clearing my throat. "I'm not usually like that," I said, hoping also to clear my name.

"You're going to be just fine," she said. "You're a tough cookie. Lucky."

I didn't feel lucky, but I felt better. Lucy and I got in a taxi and waddled up to my apartment. She guided me carefully into bed.

"Party girl," she chided, tucking the sheets in tightly.

I smiled.

"Someone's got to keep up with you," I garbled.

"I'm staying with you tonight. I'll just be hanging out in the other room. Your job is to rest. Got it?"

She looked down at me, her iridescent face appearing like an angel.

"Thanks, Lucy," I said, grasping her wrist.

She winked and I drifted off to sleep. Lucy stayed with me until she had to be at work the next day. By that time I'd healed enough to sip miso soup and pick up some pieces.

ghost

I had come to realize that I was an addict. Some people loved bands; I devoured them like a voracious animal. It was, at times, an unhealthy obsession—the polar opposite of the "everything in moderation" advice people always nod their heads to but no one seems to follow.

I hoarded music like an alcoholic to the never-empty bottle. And like a true junkie, I needed those noises to exist (my over six hundred CDs and two hundred tapes and one hundred albums proved it). But really, that now-fateful Alice in Chains chorus, sung hungrily by the late Layne Staley (R.I.P.), put it best: "What's my drug of choice? Well, what have you got?"

Cool, sold. I'll take it—*all of it.* Gulp up those notes and drizzle froth on my chin. Give me everything. I'll try it once. With that pioneering spirit in mind, I ventured out to yet another hip-hop party, this time sponsored by Elite Fleet Promotions, where none other than Tommy Hill model-socialite deejay Mark Ronson was spinning records at a new, unmarked club on Market Street called ONE. It was buried under the Manhattan Bridge like a homeless vagabond.

I was also going to try to chat up an emerging Minneapolis rapper called 7:30, who Tyran was managing. Even though I was going solo with maybe a Lucy appearance later in the evening (fingers crossed), I knew some of my industry peeps would be around. A comforting thought.

The scene outside was crazy, so instead of bum-rushing the entrance, and in a general effort to be more patient, I decided to kick back and wait in line with the common folk. Strange that parties like this one were actually crucial components of my job, I thought, as I took my position behind a b-boy and b-girl couple in matching Adidas shelltoes. Thankfully, it was a crisp, clear night so I pleasantly killed time by playing Snake on my cell phone.

The fast cars were zipping by overhead and honking sporadically. Talk about noise pollution.

Just then, I spotted a familiar groupie, standing uncomfortably in a J Chuckles top with her hands over her bare arms and her knees knocking in a short pink pleather skirt. After racking my brain, I remembered seeing her at the Jay-Z concert on Long Island the weekend before, waiting outside by the backstage entrance where all the Lincoln Continentals drove through. It was too depressing seeing her again.

I'd had a stressful day earlier of dodging phone calls from publicists pitching me "the next Tupac," dealing with an incompetent intern, and worst of all, editing a writer's interview with Eminem's ex-bodyguard (while his label had called our advertising department to express, officially, their displeasure with our doing the story). Em hated me. My home-state pride. I was as good as Moby to him.

I vowed right then to stop all that fake crap. I ditched the stagnant, predictable scene at ONE, went home, slipped into my soft pants, watched PJ Harvey be freaky and originally seductive on Conan, and flipped channels till I got sleepy.

That's when I caught a repeat of BET's new rap countdown show and there was an emcee battle segment that featured my old pal Furious, who, when it was his turn, conveniently spit a freestyle about dating a "Midwestern girl who'd never had a twirl." Sure, it was playful, but I was horrified at his public dis. Would anyone know it was me?

I became determined not to let his national exposure fade me. To never be put in a compromising work position again. It burned to feel the residue of my mistakes, but that was the price I had to pay for hanging out with spiteful dodo heads—rappers with big mouths and without boundaries. No distinction between Life and Art. I'd never let it happen to me again.

The next morning, I got a call from Eminem's people while I was smearing my everything bagel. His manager, Paul Rosenberg, agreed to do a counter story, which seemed to temporarily assuage our strained relationship and slightly redeem me with the Shady family.

Very late that night, as I lay in bed humming along to Tom Waits's "Innocent When You Dream," I had what is referred to on *Oprah* as an "Aha! moment." I realized that not only did I keep putting myself out there for guys who weren't really asking for my affection, but that the men I was picking all evoked a similar strain of emotion in me, contaminated with parallel connotations: they were boys to cast fantasies on. Fill-in-the-blanks fellas open to my interpretations.

They didn't just remind me of a song or embody a lyric or represent a sly guitar progression, they were the personification of music. Ryan had toiled as country: honest, romantic, vulnerable. Furious had been hip-hop: aggressive, offensive, raw. Jack morphed to soul: coy, seductive, elusive.

Somewhere along the crescendos and allegros and lentos and adagios, these random guys had made the music and notes and stories come alive for me—walk, breathe, talk, dance in human form.

Unfortunately, music's treasures and the comfortable distance between me and a record had been scraped. Guys were the music now. I didn't want a nasty hip-hop song or a maudlin country tune or a needy soul ballad anymore. I wanted something *real*. And for now, that something real was yours truly. So, I put away the CDs and records and tapes for the night and appreciated the silence. The serene quiet that is a blank slate. A new start. The flipside.

shut 'em down

"It's what?" I asked, clutching the phone to my ear. It felt like a car had just slammed into me. "How's that true?" I asked in disbelief.

"I know, I know," Tyran said. "Believe me, we're all in shock too."

"But it's the Mecca of rap studios," I said, already eulogizing.

"I guess everything has its end, babe. It's a new era now." His sentences sounded rehearsed, like a publicist fed them. I knew he was crushed.

"Damn," I said, feeling helpless. "Well, *BeatMaker*'s definitely gonna want a story. I'll come by this afternoon and take some notes, interview some folks. Aight?"

"That should be fine, ma. I'll tell Kevin."

I hung up the phone and sat still for a moment.

"Landmark's closing," I yelled to everyone and no one in particular.

Folks swiveled around from their screens.

"What?" Fred asked, wrinkling his nose.

"It's true, I just got the scoop," I sighed.

"Put it up on the site," said HP, lingering by my desk.

I paused. Jesus, at least let the body get cold.

"I will, in a second," I said, scratching my head, sorting out details. "I think we should head down there this afternoon and then we can crash a story into the current issue. Man, it's all going down so fast."

"I can come and shoot photos," Ethan offered.

I looked down at my watch. My head hung heavy.

"I really can't believe this. That place is like a shrine. If those walls could talk . . ." I drifted off and closed my eyes, typing out an intro 'graph in my mind.

"Let's leave in a hour or so."

Ethan nodded.

After sixty short minutes, the music world was changing right in front of my eyes. I leaned against a wall in the Landmark den and watched Ethan take pictures of an assistant pulling down plaques off the wall. I was in awe. I never for a second thought the place would go. The shapes of the vanishing awards were being maintained by all the dust that had set like shadows.

Tyran leaned with me.

"I guess we kind of knew it might happen, but it really went down after a week or so ago. It's the market crash. All of that."

I jotted down his words, trying to gauge the mood in the room. Somber, mechanical, hollow. Construction guys hauled out the pool table and video games.

"Do you think the fact that Landmark refused to update its equipment had anything to do with folks not recording here so much?"

Tyran took a moment to answer.

"I'll take the Fifth on that one."

I nodded.

"Sad day," I sighed.

"Yeah, it is. But maybe it's a sign . . . time to move on."

"I just wish they could have put Landmark in a museum or something. You know?"

Tyran smiled.

"I feel you," he said.

Groups of artists, engineers, journalists, and others converged and conversed in patches around the corridors, savoring the final moments. Someone came and tapped my shoulder.

"Hey, Sophie."

I turned around and saw Noah.

"Hey," I answered, giving him a quick hug.

He stood there, looking around the room, soaking up the scene.

"At least I got a chance to work here," he said, digging his fists into his pockets.

"Yup, you're a part of history," I said.

"True," he said. "Thanks for saying that, Sophie."

Me, Tyran, and Noah stood together shipwrecked as the last seconds of Landmark ticked by. Noah shook his head.

"I must split, fam. This shit is too sad." He kissed my cheek and gave Tyran a pound; then Ethan returned.

"I think I got some nice stuff," he said, rolling a new film into the camera.

"Me too. I got some quotes at least," I said.

"Should we get back to the offices?" he asked, checking his watch.

I nodded, said my byes to Tyran and Noah and left without asking about Furious. Outside on the curb, I looked up once more at the Landmark window and recalled the first day I walked blindly and faithfully into that studio, not knowing what I was in for, but fully aware of its legacy. Now, I'd broken off a tiny bit of my own.

When I got back to the office Fred had left a sticky note on my computer screen telling me to stop by his desk.

"Fred," I said, knocking on his open door. He swiveled around.

"Come in, Sophie, and have a seat."

Suddenly, I got butterflies in my stomach. What had I done wrong? Did my facts not check out on my "Droppin' Dime" story? Was my copy sloppy?

He just stared at me for few moments, building up my worry.

"Why do you think I called you in here?"

This felt like a trick question along the sleazy lines of "What's your greatest weakness?" I played it safe and just shrugged.

"Well," he continued. "Me, Dana, and HP got together to talk about your performance."

I had a flashback to Claire firing me from *Boldly Beautiful*. I sat up straight and crossed my legs. God, no.

"And," he said, rubbing a stack of papers on his desk. "We've decided to give you your own column."

I touched my face.

"You have?"

He nodded.

"We like your work, and we know you're passionate and committed about it."

"Uh-huh," I said.

He slid a manila envelope toward me.

"We talked about what *BeatMaker* needs right now and brainstormed a couple of ideas for you to start with. We'd like to call the column 'Heavy Rotation.'"

"I like that," I said, taking the folder into my lap.

"It'd be, like, your favorite picks and essays on hip-hop culture, relevance, artists. Get the drift?"

"Oh yeah," I said.

"Cool," he said. "Get me something to look at by Friday. Aight?"

"Okay," I said.

"Well, you better get to work then."

I took my cue and stood up.

"Thanks, Fred," I said. "I won't let you down."

He nodded.

"Good luck." He smiled.

I raced to the bathroom, locked myself into a stall and, with the folder pressed against my chest, jumped up and down in the air like a boxing champ. I won, I mouthed, I won!

up in smoke

You know how people in relationships say it's the minute you let your guard down that you'll land the man of your dreams? Once, I'd hated those people. Saying blasé things like, "The moment when you least expect it, he'll come along like some prince on horseback emerging from the thick forest." I'd been forced to write a positive story about those annoying people in *Boldly Beautiful* once—one of those "don't lose hope" pieces. As if society could—no, *would*—ever let a single girl have the pleasure of forgetting she's alone!

Post-interviewing those obnoxious happy couples and working on that article, I was brainwashed. I went around dropping off dry cleaning, alphabetizing my CDs, ironing my pants, shirts, undies, all in an effort to distract myself from that one dream—Him. I'd go to Barnes & Noble and force myself not to eye the guy in Autobiographicals or buy flowers at the deli and try not to look over my shoulder in line. I'd try to force myself out of thinking I'd found love, but he just hadn't found me yet.

Still, I couldn't stop obsessing about the day or way it might happen. I also couldn't imagine ever forgetting that he was somewhere out there, maybe under my nose or on the other side of the world or on a corner hailing a cab. Until the day I actually did give up, surrendered, and let go. I was tired of searching. Guys had confused and hurt me right into submission. I put down my weapons and waved the white flag. The battle was over, I'd lost.

This is the exact moment a girl has to be on guard, but like most of the defeated, I was chillin' on my couch wearing a clay mask, eating M&Ms and popcorn, and watching a Lifetime movie when I got the call. I thought it was Mom pestering me about holiday plans, so I let the phone ring a few times and picked up in no hurry.

"You've reached *The Bell Jar*. Please make this good."

I expected her to start laughing or feeling sorry for me (both acceptable reactions), but instead I heard a male voice clearing his throat.

"Ma?"

"Whoa. What was that all about?"

"Fred?" I couldn't recognize the voice.

"Who's Fred?"

I sat up straight on the couch. My mask was solidifying, drying me up.

"Jack."

"You're lucky I like you," he said and, thank God, let out a laugh. "I was number three on that list."

"I'm sorry. I just didn't think it'd be you."

"I feel really special now."

"Look, cut it out. What's up?"

"Nothing, I just wanted to see. Say. See what you were doing tomorrow night?"

"Do you always just call people out of the blue?"

He laughed. "That's my strategy. I'm a surpriser."

"Did your girlfriend cancel on you or something?"

"Ha-ha. Yeah, I probably deserve that but actually no, I got an extra ticket to the 'Up in Smoke' show and since you're the hip-hop queen . . ."

I debated. It seemed sketchy that it was so last minute but at least he'd thought of me. Maybe he was making an effort. A grand gesture?

"Hello?" he asked.

"I'm here," I replied. "I just wanted to leave you in suspense for a moment."

"Thanks, Sophie. I know I can always count on you."

"Yeah, I'll go. I've never seen any of those cats before."

"Cool. I hope you want to see me too, not just Dr. Dre."

"Errr," I grumbled. "Fine, I do."

We met outside the *BeatMaker* offices at six. Jack approached me in a D.A.R.E. T-shirt and a new fauxhawk.

"I like the shirt," I said, pecking his cheek. "You make me laugh."

"You look pretty," he said, taking in my new Sergio Valente jeans and striped top.

"What's the flyer in your hand?"

"I just got it. It's some hip-hop and snowboarding festival up in Vermont."

He snatched the paper from me and read it.

"Who you taking to that?"

I shrugged.

"I don't even know if I'll go."

He gave me back the paper and I stuffed it into my purse.

We crossed the street holding hands, picking our relationship up right where we left off, and making our way to the LIRR.

"I wanted to talk to you, Sophie," he said, facing me backward on the train.

"Okay," I said, lying back. "About what?"

"Jenny and I are breaking up—officially."

"That's a shocker," I said, acting bitchy.

"C'mon now, I'm trying to be real here."

I apologized.

The train accelerated out of the tunnel, launching us into a postcard-perfect view of the skyline.

"I want to know if you think we might be able to date?"

I felt like he was asking his leading questions for informational purposes only again, but I didn't care. I was worn out.

"Yes," I answered in complete truth. "I'm crazy about you."

He leaned forward to me.

"I know," he answered, pulling a Han Solo.

I shook my head.

"I take it back."

He squeezed my knee.

"I want to be with you, too."

"Then you can't be with Jenny," I said. "Or any other girl," I added, clearing up any polyamorous confusion.

"I know," he said, sitting back and gazing out the window. He began chewing his cuticles and I started to doubt my being honest with him. Maybe he couldn't take it. Maybe he'd never completely sever their ties. And worst of all, maybe I wasn't the One.

"Let's have fun tonight," he said.

"Yes, let's declare the funness begins now," I pounded my thigh.

He leaned in and kissed me and I really did feel like a queen then.

"Don't waste my time again, Jack."

He shook his head, cradling my hand in between his palms.

At the show, we waved our hands in the air to Dre, Em, and Snoop. We rapped and sang along so much our voices were hoarse. We soothed our ailing throats with Bud Lights. We made out to "Gin & Juice." Jack bought a souvenir "tobacco pipe" which we played with on the train. I discovered he could do a killer Sherlock Holmes impression. We laughed our asses off. He went all the way home with me, but I wouldn't let him go all the way once we were home.

I stopped him at the stoop of my building.

"I had fun with you tonight, but we're not getting together yet," I said, pressing my palm on his chest. It took everything for me to get that out. "I'm probably going to that thing in Vermont this weekend, but if we're going to do this, you're going to have to pursue me. Make the effort. Make up for the past." I wiggled my eyebrows.

"I know," he said.

I hugged him, took in his musky scent and the feel of his familiar frame pressed against me. I was scared to let him go, but I knew I had to.

"I'll be in touch with you."

I nodded skeptically but wanted to believe. My well of faith in him was as-yet undrainable.

"Okay, Jack. Do that." I turned away from him and ran up the stairs before weakness took over and I changed my mind about inviting him in. When I got inside my apartment, I ran in the dark to the window, where I watched him cross the street and disappear around the corner. I prayed he might find his way back to me. (It was almost summer now and anything seemed possible again.)

getting grown

At work the next afternoon, I RSVP'd late for "Mt. NYC," the imminent hip-hop and snowboarding weekend in Vermont. The publicist for the event, who I knew from his old PR position at Rawkus, two-wayed me back instantly with a friendly message that he was happy to hear that I was attending and that I'd be getting first dibs for interview slots. This made me bust out a smile.

I'd never been to the East Coast's mountains, so I thought this would be the perfect reason to head out of the city and pollution—work, play, and rest. Online, I booked a roundtrip train and a single room at the Red Rob Inn.

When I got up there late on Thursday night, Killington appeared like a quaint alpine village. I plopped down into my toasty room, slapped some Gang Starr into my laptop, and logged online to file a story for deadline and review the event agenda. I read that the next day was a free day with press registration and a pro demo in the afternoon and a hip-hop show with some East Coast deejay and emcees that night at the Base Lodge. I was going to hit the slopes in the a.m. before I had to report for registration at the tents.

When I left my room that morning with my board, layers of clothes on, and headphones wrapped around my neck, I noticed a group of high school kids doing doughnuts in the back parking lot behind the inn. In one black SUV, there was a teenage boy and girl giggling like mad and spinning around and around in the snow. I stepped into the shade so they wouldn't notice me watching.

He drove them fearlessly in circles and I could tell by the way the young girl was clutching the boy's shoulder that she was scared. She laughed anyway, like she couldn't help it because the ride was so thrilling. Or maybe the momentum was so great that it tickled her. Or maybe she just wanted to impress him. Those were her secrets.

He manned the wheel, twisting his arms over one another rapidly, getting off on being out of control. From the stairs I was standing on, their recklessness seemed to make perfect sense, their relationship a giant amusement park, a scene from the perfect pop song.

I walked down to the shuttle bus, shuffling over the rocks and dirty ice in my giant boots. I got to the snowshed and took my board up to the lift. It was a couple centimeters too big but I'd gotten it on sale and figured I'd grow into it. I strapped one foot on, shimmying up to the gate and snapping my minty gum.

The lift operator was cute—medium-rare pink cheeks and an easy grin.

"Have a good run," he said, guiding the chair underneath me like a swing. I looked over my shoulder and waved thanks.

On the way up to mid-mountain, the whole world seemed still except for the clean sounds of folks slicing through the fresh snow on skis and boards below and the steady creak of the lift inching its way along. Patches of powder balanced on the branches of the trees, glittery sprinkles of delicate snowflakes.

I swung my free foot and tapped it gently against my Burton Charger. I thought about New York and hip-hop and the boys that came with my life, woven into its fabric over the time I'd been there—and even the ones I hadn't met yet. This made my eyes water so I wiped them with my glove. It all seemed so very far away from where I was, like a distant, urban fairy-tale land that I'd escaped from. Suddenly, time seemed to elapse and catch up to me with the whip of the wind.

I rewound the mixtape I'd brought with me for the morning. I'd made it a year ago when I had first moved to New York and met Jack, completely re-entering a wicked West Coast rap phase. From DJ Quik to Dilated, Dre to Planet Asia and People Under The Stairs. The tape was screeching backward.

I didn't know all the answers of what had happened to me in the city, or what effect I might have had on the people I met, but I felt pretty sure that as time went on, so would I. And that I wouldn't forget or hang on too tight as I moved away from the drama. Mostly, I felt relieved to know that it was over and I'd survived intact. I was better for it and maybe those guys carried some fond memories of me.

I'd also recently found that crinkled "Things I Love Most" list stuffed into a pair of socks at home, so I brought it with me and slipped it into a side pocket on my Roxy pants. Amazingly, it still rang one hundred percent true. And yet, after a year in New York, I felt one hundred percent changed.

I jumped off the lift, put my fluorescent orange goggles down, and popped my earphones in place. Then I decided that maybe this morning, I'd take the second lift all the way up to the summit, higher than I'd ever been. I didn't feel completely ready but I thought, what the hell, I could give it a shot, discover a new trail.

So I inched along to the lift, reminding myself (and my scared belly) that the first time was always the hardest, beginning was the worst. Then, I wasn't worried about falling or where the trail might lead or bumping into other people on the path or where I'd end up at the bottom. Because, chances were, I'd live and there'd be more opportunities to improve. That's what this sport was all about, after all: determination and progression and individuality.

My brand-new, comped Motorola cell rang somewhere in my board pants. I tore open the many Velcro pockets up and down my legs. I didn't recognize the number when I flipped open the phone and spoke. It felt like I was really swinging on the chair lift now.

" 'Ello," I said, affecting a British accent and catching bits of wet snow in my mouth. The altitude was getting to my head and making me silly. Sillier.

"Sophie, it's Jack."

I wiped my nose on my glove. I was now beyond accustomed to his back-n-forth game of tag.

"Jack? Hey."

"I have something I need to talk to you about."

"Okay, I'm kind of in the middle of something right now though." I looked out on the horizon where people were hopping off the lift and disappearing into the whiteness. I sensed something hollow in his voice, a breeze.

"Where are you calling from?" I heard my voice echo somewhere and turned around. There he was, in the chair right behind me. This was a dream. I'd had this dream.

"I guess you didn't want me to wait long," I said into the phone. I watched him mouth his reply in a short time delay.

"Didn't want to risk it," he said.

I fixed my eyes on him.

"You know, you'll never reach me from there."

He nodded, outstretching his arms as we creaked along.

"Don't worry, I'll catch up. I'll getcha," he said.

"I can't believe you found me." I shook my head and looked down at the mountain. "You ready?"

"All yours," he nodded.

"I gotta warn you that I'm not very good at traversing yet."

"That's okay. I'll help you improve," he said.

I turned away from him and saw the DANGER sign warning riders to lift their safety bar.

"Ready or not," I said to Jack and snapped the phone shut.

He hopped off after me. We stopped and he kissed my cheek while we sat in the snow. Folks were weaving around us. I couldn't stop smiling.

"I'll watch you," he said. "Take off first and we'll meet at the bottom. Freestyle it."

"I'm not that graceful," I warned.

He shrugged.

"So, my form's shit," he confessed.

"And I'm slow," I said.

"I don't care, Sophie."

"One question." I couldn't stop interviewing people.

He nodded.

"Are you leaving tonight or staying on?"

"You're not getting rid of me now," he said.

"Good," I answered. "'Cause I'm definitely going to need a massage later."

He laughed.

I finagled myself to my feet and regained my balance.

"Here goes nothing," I said, slipping away.

"Go big," Jack cheered, making a megaphone with his hands.

I heaved myself off the mountain's edge, knowing right then that I'd make it down just fine.

By Sunday, Jack and I were headed back to the city together in his blue Dodge Colt. When we neared Manhattan, the sky broke and the sun peeked out for a moment over the skyline. I looked over at Jack as the light swept across his face—tiny peach fuzz glowing on his sunburned cheeks. He glanced over and smiled at me. I smiled back. DJ Shadow's "What Does Your Soul Look Like" was playing on the radio.

"I love this song," I said, under my breath.

"Me too," said Jack, nodding.

I reached for the knob and turned the volume up as loud as it would go. Until the speakers shook and so did we. Everything seemed to come together in that moment—New York, Jack, hip-hop—even me.

the extras

INTERVIEW 1 ● slick rick

written by Giselle Wasfie

slick rick

"Hauk, who goes yonder?

It is I, sire, Richard of Nottingham.

Well, speak up, man, what is it?

News from the east, sire, Rick the Ruler has returned!"

—THE RULER'S BACK

Slick Rick is the ruler. And he's coming back to reclaim his rap kingdom. Although his new album is still mostly a vision, the potential and anticipation are huge. Now he's letting you be a part of the dream with his *Online Producer Project with Def Jam.* SOHH caught up with the smoothed-out rap legend to talk about the new joint, his double-duty as a Bronx landlord and how he wrote classics like "Mona Lisa" and "Children's Story." Same honeyed voice with a touch of a British accent, same Slick Rick we all know and love!

How has Hip-Hop changed since you got in the game?

I think it's become more advanced in terms of concepts, the raps are more skillful, advanced. There's a lot more gangsta rap. In general, there's a lot more appreciation for rap. When we started people said rap might be a passing phase. Now there are movies, major rap jingles in Pepsi commercials and it's much more mainstream.

What do you think about these changes?
I think they're pretty much positive. It's open more horizons for rappers if you have genuine skills. The negative is that there's a lot of gangsta orientated rap and ra ra. There's some cleaning up that has to happen today.

What do you think about artists who use your work as influence (like Snoop Doggy Dogg and "La Di Da Di"?)
It's an honor. You feel like you've made an impression on this generation. You realize your work wasn't in vain—your stories, humor, etcetera, etcetera.

What's it like working on the new album?
It's like more upscale, not like wealth-centered. It's to entertain an older crowd—topics that pertain to a person with kids, married, working—it's not necessarily for kids in high school. It's topics of whatever we go through at 30 and sh*t like that—a mortage, a woman . . . topics that adults think about. It's genuine entertainment for an adult, but it's not preachy. I wanna make records that are not too silly; records that have more substance.

What's a typical day like for Slick Rick?
Well, now, I'm pretty much anxious about my new album. I also have a couple of buildings in the Bronx that me and my mom

purchased. So, I tend to them, they're like two/three family joints.

How do folks react to having Slick Rick as their landlord?
(Laughs) They're cool but some people do trip off the fact!

Where is the new album at now?
We're in the beginning phases. I had an idea that I ran by my label that besides getting a bunch of producers together we'd run the Internet thing . . .

You're talking about the online producer?
It'll probably catch on. I got the idea because I call tracks "Writing Paper" that I put my voice over. I'm looking for good writing paper. I get to pick.

What's your favorite Slick Rick song?
I like "Children's Story." It's lively and still makes me dance and have fun. I like the song I did with OutKast too.

Who do you like in rap now?
I like OutKast—I like one track here and there from lots of artists like Busta Rhymes, Method Man, R. Kelly, lotta different people.

Who else do you listen to?
I listen to the classic songs that have an emotional sound to them. I like the Beatles. I like real soulful songs that made number one.

I like composing a whole song. Almost like writing a beginning, topic and ending . . . almost like an essay.

Like with "Children's Story," the beginning talks about how robbery is bad, and then I'm going to tell you why, and then I told a story of a kid who did it and this is why you shouldn't.

How'd you write "Mona Lisa"?
That was something more like I liked the track and just wrote anything on it. I just wrote and wrote and continued, continued and it turned out to be a nice, hot track.

Are there any producers you're wanting to work with?
There are a lotta great producers out there. I just want all my tracks to be good tracks. Everyone knows who the big dogs is and I already know. I'll definitely step to them too, but I just want a good track to rhyme on and I don't care who gives it to me.

INTERVIEW 2 • nelly

written by Giselle Wasfie

At the tender age of 24, Nelly's now sold over 10 million albums. In 2000, he got everyone crunk with his *Country Grammar* and two years later, he's keeping the summer sweaty and sexy with his Neptunes club-banger, "Hot in Herre," from his recent sophomore effort, *Nellyville*, which within a month has already gone Triple Platinum. Read here to find out about how one kid from St. Louis launched a rap phenomenon, what's really up with that Band-Aid and how Nelly manages to keep his cool through it all!

Did you really come out of nowhere with Country Grammar *or have you been in it for a minute?*
Me and the group [St. Lunatics] been together since '93. We all grew up listening to hip-hop, feelin' it, it was the thing to do, but not like now. Now, if you're a kid and you're not listening to hip-hop, something is wrong with you socially. (Laughs) I mean, it don't have to be your main form of music, don't get me wrong, but you are aware of it, you are listening to it in some shape or form. And that's just how it's been.

People seem to be fascinated that you're from St. Louis. What was the Hip-Hop scene like there growing up?
Well, it wasn't a real heavy hip-hop scene, you know, just what was more or less mainstream. Not like an underground scene like it is today. Or like it's existed like the last ten years on. We had . . . on the radio the hot tracks, not like now though where tracks like might not actually be in rotation or tracks that might just get played in one state or real local artists getting local airplay. You get local airplay for artists in St. Louis and out the Midwest, closer to your airplay. Now stations don't just play what's hot, the Billboard top 20, top 50, top 200, but also to play what's locally hot, because hip-hop is now so big and because of the audience that it attracts.

Well, the eyes weren't on that area of the country for a while.
I think that's why we do as well as we do. Because we be from new places, new sounds, untapped areas. Once we do come out, it's like they're more into the place, as well, not just the music. You might be a new artist out New York, and people be like, they hot. But, you not that into where he came from because numerous people came from. Same with L.A.

Do you feel there are lots of expectations on you now?
I think people are just waiting to see, you can't expect nobody to repeat nine, ten million albums. Maybe I'm saying that 'cause I'm in the business, but to an average fan they might really know the difference. I didn't really know about record sales before I got into it, I'd just see a video on TV and I'd see the man on there, I'm already thinking he sold all these records, I mean, why wouldn't he? That's

kind of like how the average person might look at it. But nobody expecting me to repeat stuff like that, but just perform well. If I can do half of it, two-fourths, believe me, it's a lot better than a lot of other artists.

How did you refine your flow? And when did your passion for music turn into something you wanted to do for a living?

Well, when you first start rapping, it's never how you end up rapping. I mean, your first flow, you basically trying to find yourself, trying to get comfortable on the mic, comfortable in studio, what you do. When you do finally find a little form or what it is you feel comfortable doing, that's what you run with. Then, that's what it took for me. Once I found it, I was like, okay, this is it right here. This flow, this is how I feel comfortable. This is what I want to do. It just came about—being comfortable on the mic and trying to be distinct and different at the same time . . . doing something nobody else doing.

Once you found your comfortable point. Did you notice people's responses?

I saw them appreciate it more. People were just like "that's tight" or "nobody did that" or "how'd you do that? That's raw," whatever the case. You just can't be scared to do it though. See that's the thing, I think some people get scared because it's never been done before, they don't want to do it or try it and then it's too late after someone else tried it, now it's his. You gotta get out there and go with the flow. You know, individually. People might be scared that they'll stick out if they try something different and be judged, so they come in being like somebody else, which might work and they might even get on, but eventually you're still going to be known as the man that sounds like him.

What's some practical advice you can give someone who wants to rap professionally?

First, just make sure that's what you really wanna do because it's going to take everything you've got. 'Cause there gonna be times where it's gonna look like it's not gonna happen. There's gonna be times where it looks like it's gonna happen and it don't. There's gonna be let-downs, gonna be buildups, and it's the people that can suck that up and go to the next level. Them the ones who make it through. Ain't no overnight progress, ain't no overnight success, none of that. It's a steady build.

Don't get me wrong, you have had people who just out the blue, get a deal for whatever reason but you haven't earned that deal. When you earn it, you take it more seriously, than if one day somebody heard you sing in the mall, you never thought about singing before and they was like, you should have a record deal. That kind of stuff don't happen, I'm not saying that it hasn't or won't, but it don't happen on the regular. And if that's not your case, you're going to have to work on it.

Or there are people that are just out for that first deal and don't think long-term . . .

Well, they don't know how hard it is. They just see this [what's up front]. They don't see behind the scenes. They don't know

I been up since like eight in the morning doing interviews . . . (Laughs)

Or that you gotta eat your piece of pizza while you talk to me . . .
(Laughs) Yeah, they don't know that. You get up and you're rollin'. . . . constantly. You got your photo shoots, and your videos and your constant travel. And that's just the business, that's not even family, that's not even friends, or trying to deal with other aspects of the game—that's just the music. That's not the clothing, movie-thing or label you're trying to get started. That's none of that, that's just your album. So, it's hard, it's hard.

Sounds tiring.
It's work though. And that's why not everybody can be where you're at and that's why everybody can't do it cause it's like that. It's the ones that pull through; if it's gotta be done, it's gotta be done.

What do you love about what you do?
It's the people, just the fans. To run up onstage and having like 30,000 people just screaming their heads off, at the top of their lungs, like "yo, tell us what to do and we gonna do it!" Just being up there, I think that's the best. Cause you know, the show is like me showing appreciation. You getting up onstage and I'm showing you I appreciate you spending that fourteen, fifteen dollars for the CD. That $30, 35, 55—whatever the ticket price—that poster you got, all them posters. This is what I do. I appreciate it. So, it's definitely the fans.

Not to oversimplify, but your songs are just so damn catchy. How do you write them?
I don't know. That's always been a plus for me. I've been fortunate that I can have people catch on pretty quickly. I'm finding out that . . . that everybody can write a hot sixteen, but not everybody can make a complete song. Everybody can make a complete song, but can't make a complete album. So, we've been fortunate enough, that we've been able to do all that. And I just try to go with the flow man, I just do what the beat tells me to do. I think my thing is, I don't try to overpower the beat or force some flow on the beat. Every flow don't go right on every beat and I don't force it. I try to add to the beat, like instrument-wise, as well as my flow as well as saying something and I try to keep those things in mind while I'm writing. Fortunately enough, everything done turned out well.

Tell people about your new album—Nellyville.
June 25th. It's kinda funny 'cause you get your whole life to plan your first album, then after you do that, you only get like a year and some months to do your second one. So, it's kind of hard to really hard to say . . . like with the first album to be in the same place and have those same feelings. I'm not sitting here to just write sixteens all day long, like some people, and then just put a hook in between them all and call them a song. You know, I don't do that. If I'm gonna make song, I'm gonna make a song on that topic, what's goin' on. Don't get me wrong, I have wrote a sixteen and added it to a song, but that's not my main focus on how I got into attacking a song. During *Nellyville,* I'm just trying to show everybody a place, through the lyrics and paint you a picture, as far as everything I go

through now. Things I've experienced, the things I appreciate about what's going on, what I don't appreciate, just my life as a whole now. Just do it right, the same way I've been doing it, the Nelly-way.

Like I say, if you been rollin' with me now, everybody who ain't rollin' with me, they done jumped off the bandwagon by now. So, I already did something you didn't like by now—the Jagged Edge thing or the 'N Sync thing—I don't know (Laughs), if I did something, so you gone by now so I ain't got nothing but the people who rollin' with me. And the people who rollin' with me, I think are really gonna love this album. I think they'll really feel it and be happy with it. You know, I'm happy with it and everybody around me happy with it so . . . I think they'll be happy.

One last question, what the hell's up with the Band-Aid on your cheek?
It was like Memorial Day weekend and I was in Miami and you know, I'm wylin', I'm playing basketball with everybody else. You know, I get popped and I get a cut and my first instinct is to put a Band-Aid on it. I didn't think nothing of it. I'm not trying to make a significant statement with it or nothing, I'm just like where's a Band-Aid? Okay, whatever, let's go back out.

I had to go do photo shoots, interviews, whatever. When you got that many people watching you, it's crazy how somebody pick up on what you do. One day, I could be writing with my right hand, then the next day I'm writing with my left and a fan might see that and be like, "you're not left-handed!" (Laughs) So, I'm either a Nelly-fake at this point or something. And you know, it goes on, it don't stop—interviews, photo shoots, videos, award shows—and you just go with it. Now, I got kids running up to me with five or six Band-Aids stuck to their face and moms coming to me complaining about how her son is in the medicine cabinet with all the Band-Aids and is ripping up the tape or whatever . . . (Laughs)

That's some power you got there.
Yeah, it's a beautiful thing.

INTERVIEW 3 • eminem's camp

written by Giselle Wasfie

In the controversial book *Shady Bizzness,* Eminem's ex-bodyguard, Byron "Big Nasty" Williams talks about life on the road with the controversial, multi-platinum phenom—groupies, guns and Kim. Here, Marshall Mathers's friend and fellow D-12 rapper, Proof, and Em's former road manager, Dee Tee, tell you their behind-the-scenes stories

—FROM BIG NASTY TO EM, KIM TO GROUPIES, AND MORE.

big nasty

Proof:

His stories are filled with very exaggerated details. I've known Em for twelve years, he doesn't wake up and eat Ecstasy with his eggs—that just makes a good, interesting story, but it's not true. Big only knew us for ten months and now he's just out to hurt Em and make money. He wanted to be a rapper and he's upset. Big doesn't mention any of the stuff he did out on the road—like video-taping girls . . . He wasn't a mentor to Em; they weren't boys. Em doesn't feel betrayed 'cause that sh!t is not true. Big's just a down man trying to make some money. He used to ask for raises every month and Em gave him anything he wanted and then Big quit on him.

Dee Tee:

At the core, Nasty's a good-hearted guy, but now he's just out to pay some bills. He was always about money. The first time I met him, he was asking for more money from Paul. That story about Em testing him by jumping into crowds is bullsh!t. Nasty wasn't Em's big brother figure. Nasty was like a "glorified groupie" who wasn't even good at being a bodyguard. Now he's just sh!tting on people and betraying Em.

Groupies

Proof:

That "underage" girl in Sweden was missing and we got checked for her, but she wasn't with us. Kessia was a friend. We've met a lot of people on tour; they follow us to different shows and we get to know them, but they're just cool with us.

Dee Tee:

Em did not sleep around like that. He would pass out after shows, or have a pizza, he wasn't interested in all that other sh!t. Girls were in every city and he can get women. That story about me and Em in Pittsburgh—Nasty has no idea what went on. There were girls there, but it wasn't an orgy. And I stayed behind, Em left.

Kim

Proof:

Em and Kim are trying to work things out. Their relationship is still up in the air. They're going through their things, but they love each other. There are many wonderful things to say about Kim. People only see one side. Couples have fights, but people don't know what conversations happen in their bedrooms. Em loves his family. A lot of it is just typical "baby mama drama." That song "Kim" on the Marshall Mathers EP was supposed to be on the first album. He wrote that song way back when he was broke and struggling and he had pressure to pay bills and Kim was asking him to sacrifice his dreams, but many people go through that pressure.

Dee Tee:

Kim is basically a nice woman whose had a hard life. And Em talks about beating her in those songs, but really she could beat him if she wanted—she's a bit taller than him and she's a tough woman. I think they really do love each other.

Paul Rosenberg (Em's Manager):

Proof:

The reason that Em knows Paul is because of me. We all have skills on the mic, but Paul sacrificed his dream and went to school and became a lawyer and that contributes to all of us. We all trust Paul and he doesn't make any decisions for Em. Me and Paul have known Em for years and we would get Em's back, he knows that.

Dee Tee:

Paul was just doing his job. Working for Eminem is still work. It's still business. Yes, Paul decides what people make, but that's what he's supposed to do. He decided my salary. Paul and Em are caring employers.

Eminem

Proof:

He's still the simplest man in the world. He still feels like he could fall off tomorrow. His head hasn't blown up. Em just reacts to people who initiate it. He's also gullible sometimes. Dre told him to have security people sign papers that said they wouldn't write books about him, but Em didn't want to do that. Now, he's learned he has to do those things to protect his family. He feels like he's given so much to his career and all of a sudden, Hailie will be, like, ten years-old. We're cutting our next tour short, so he can come home. He's going to do the D-12 album, a couple of movies, and then retire from rap.

Dee Tee:

He's a genius and he has a good crew. On the road, he'd be writing rhymes like he didn't have a record deal. He's competitive, hungry and talented. Em's daughter is his life.